Always Yours

Whiskey Men

Hope Ford

Chapter 1

Ally

I stretch my hand across my belly and look around the low-lit room. The music is loud, people are relaxing, trying to relieve the stress of their week, and I'm sitting here completely on edge. I shouldn't be here, but as I look over at Natalie, I do feel better that I'm not the only one here in this condition.

She leans over to yell into my ear. "We have babies... in a bar."

She pulls back, laughing and rubbing her expansive belly. I know we're both thinking of that popular movie from years ago where the woman was holding her baby in a bar. However, neither Natalie nor I have had our babies yet. Nope, I still have three months to go, and Natalie has four months before her baby is due.

I grab on to her wrist and shift on the bar stool. "I can't believe I let you talk me into this. I shouldn't be here. I should be at home with my swollen feet propped up and trying to rest. Isn't that what people say? Sleep before the baby comes."

She shrugs her shoulders and scrunches her nose up. "No, I think the saying is to sleep when the baby is sleeping. And I talked you into this because you can't keep hiding out. No one cares about your circumstances. At least not like you think."

And at that moment, my body physically jerks from the kick of the baby. Wow, that was a good one. I run my hand over my belly soothingly. "I haven't been hiding out."

But as soon as the words are out, I know I'm lying. "Fine, you wanted me out, I'm out. But I didn't think we'd be meeting at my ol' hangout."

The Whiskey Whistler is a popular hangout, and I've been coming here since the day I turned twenty-one. Basically everyone comes here that wants to unwind in Whiskey Run.

Natalie reaches for me and wraps her hand around mine. Her touch calms me, and I'm sure it's because we're going through the same thing. Well, sort of. We're both pregnant, but where she's married and secure in her relationship, I'm single and have no one. Well, I have Austin. He's my best friend who would literally do anything for me, but it's not quite the same. Natalie's husband Beau is one of Austin's older brothers, and I'm pretty sure that Austin convinced Natalie to drag me out tonight. I hold back a sigh, not giving in to the pity party I want to have right now. "Okay, so how does this work?"

Olivia, Chloe, Abby, and Natalie all look at me. Olivia is smiling ear to ear as she pulls the book from her bag and holds it up with a big grin on her face. "Did you read it?"

I'm about to answer her when Abby gasps, grabbing the book out of her hands and then slamming it face down on the table between us. She's looking around the bar to see if anyone saw it before glaring at Olivia. "Why do you do that? Why? I swear, I think you do it just so you can embarrass me." She waves her hand toward the rest of us. "Yes, we all read it. We don't have to get the book out to talk about it. We don't need the whole town to know what we read."

I lean in and try to hear over the bar sounds. At least it's not a night where they have live music. This place would be packed, and we wouldn't be able to hear anything. But even for six o'clock in the evening, it's louder than normal.

Olivia rolls her eyes and pries the book out of Abby's hands. "You are such a prude. This one was good. I was impressed."

Abby shakes her head. "There was way too much sex and not enough plot."

Natalie turns to me. "What did you think, Ally? Did you like it?"

My face heats but not for the reason that Abby's did. No, I thought the book was good, and yes, there was a lot of sex, but I thought it added to the story. Nope, the reason I'm embarrassed to talk about it is because I couldn't help but read the story and think about my own best friend. "It was good. I love the friends to lovers trope, though. It's one of my favorites."

Chloe chimes in for the first time. "Duh! We all could have guessed that."

I shift on the seat again. I swear my ass has doubled in size because this seat feels way smaller than normal. I take the lemon off my glass and squeeze it into my water. I'm trying to think of a retort, but all I can do is stick my tongue out at her.

All my friends laugh, and thankfully, Olivia starts talking about the book, leaving me off the hook.

I only joined the book club a few weeks ago, but I am already loving it. The past few months I've spent way too much of my time at my house on the couch. It's only after months of doing the same thing night after night, having both Natalie and Austin nag me, that I decided I needed to get my shit together.

I was hiding out. I live in a small town, I'm pregnant, and I'm not married. I've waited for the people in town to talk about me. I've waited for the stares or the righteous people to tell me everything I'm doing wrong, but it hasn't happened yet. If anything, everyone in town has been really supportive. Of course, it doesn't hurt that my best friend is Austin Blaze. No one is going to go against a Blaze. At least no one around here.

The server comes and starts setting out appetizers. Every empty spot on the table is soon filled with french fries, mozzarella sticks, chicken wings, and potato skins. She takes the last item off the tray and sets it in front of me. "And last but not least, a grilled chicken salad with ranch on the side."

Natalie groans and points her fork at my food. "Good for you, but I'm going to enjoy all this fried, cheesy goodness."

I look at the little plate she's filling from the appetizers and I'm instantly jealous. I would love to eat that, but I've already been warned by my doctor that I needed to rein it in because my blood pressure is high. My last visit, I had a ten-minute talk on the importance of nutrition, so to avoid bed rest and other ailments, I'm doing my best to eat what he recommended. Especially since I have a follow-up appointment tomorrow.

"Congratulations, by the way."

My fork is midair, and I try not to tense at the server's words. I look at her name tag and read the name there. I see her in here all the time. Heck, I'm pretty sure she's helped me out a time or two, even holding my hair the night I turned twenty-one all those years ago. She's smiling at me, and it looks sincere. I run my hand along my belly. "Thank you, Megan."

Her forehead creases. "Oh, I mean congratulations on the baby too, but I meant on your engagement. I hear you're marrying Austin."

I sit up a little taller. I can feel everyone at the table staring at me, waiting for my response. I never talk about my relationship with Austin, but obviously it's been on everyone's minds. "Oh, uh, thank you, but—"

Natalie leans into me, resting her head on my

shoulder. "We're going to be sisters, and our kids are going to be cousins. I mean, how cool is that?"

I force a laugh even though what I really want to do is roll my eyes. Natalie knows that Austin and I are not getting married. She is married to Austin's older brother, and she knows that Austin and I are just friends. Well, I shouldn't say just friends. Truth is, we've been best friends since we were in middle school so yeah, over half our lives. I thank the server again, and when she walks away and is out of hearing range, I turn to Natalie. All eyes are on me still, but I address my friend. "You know that Austin and I are not getting married." I cup my hand across my belly. "Just like you know that this baby is not Austin's."

She gasps as if I've said something awful when I'm only speaking the truth. "Ally, don't say that."

I lean toward her. "Why? It's true. I'm not marrying Austin, and this baby is not his. I don't know why he insists—"

I cut myself off because I don't even know what to think anymore. I got pregnant, and the dad wants nothing to do with me or the baby. I waited to tell Austin, because I know how he is. Any time I ever have a problem, he fixes it. In my mind, this wasn't something he could fix. Or so I thought, anyway. It was barely out of my mouth before he told me, "You and I are getting married." And then he pointed at my then flat belly and said, "And that baby is ours now."

I argued with him, and quite honestly, I've always gotten my way with Austin. It's a common joke around his family that if any of them want something from him, they go through me to get it. But this was not something I could talk him out of. From the day I told him, he has said we are getting married and having a baby.

It's only when I shake my head from being lost in thought that I realize all my friends are looking at me. Olivia is the first one to speak. "Okay, so you're telling me that the baby's father wants nothing to do with you or the baby?"

Natalie swats her friend on the arm and admonishes her. "Olivia!"

I drop my fork on the napkin beside my salad. I know she doesn't mean anything by it. I've been around Olivia enough to know that she just says it like it is. We work in the same salon, and even though we've never really hung out together outside of work until recently, I do know how she is. "No, it's okay. Yes, Olivia, that's right. Gregory, the biological father, doesn't want me or the baby."

She nods and leans forward. "So your best

friend, who I mean, let's forget the fact that he is a Blaze and one of the richest men in the state for right now, but your best friend wants to marry you and wants to claim your child as his own. Is that right? Are the rumors true?"

I gulp, staring at Olivia wide-eyed while jutting my chin at her. "Yes, that's true."

She creases her forehead, staring at me. The place may be full of people, but right now, I'm only focused on the women at my table, staring at me as if I've lost my mind. I know they think I'm crazy. I'm sure they all know that I don't have any family to depend on and I live on the other side of town in a trailer park. I'm sure they know that I don't fit in with Natalie or any of the rest of the Blaze family. Under the intense scrutiny, all I can do is ramble. "Look, yeah, of course he offered to help me. That's what Austin does. He's a helper. Since the day we met in middle school, he's been there for me, so of course he thinks he has to be the one to fix this. But I'm not going to punish him for the rest of our lives by forcing him to be with me. He doesn't want to be married to me…. He definitely doesn't want to be the father to some other man's child. No, I'm not doing it. I won't."

By the time my rant is over, I'm wiping at the

tear on my cheek, half disgusted with myself. I'm stronger than this. I don't cry, but these stupid pregnancy hormones have me doing all kinds of crazy things.

Nat wraps her hand around mine, offering me comfort, and Olivia raises her hand, palm out to me. "I'm sorry, Ally. I know this is none of my business, and I should stay out of it. But can I ask you one thing?"

I shrug my shoulders, still on the defensive. It's not like whatever she's about to ask me is going to make me feel any worse.

She takes a deep breath. "This is all I'm going to say and then I'll stay out of it. First of all, we're all on your side. I know you're new to the group, but you're one of us, and unfortunately that means you're going to get my opinion even when it's not what you want to hear."

I nod as my heart picks up a little. I know I'm not really one of them, but it's nice to hear nonetheless.

"The other thing is, I've seen you two together at the shop and here. We've seen you with Austin... and we've seen the way he looks at you. You may think he's doing this because of his need to look out for you, but there's more to it than that." She leans forward. "All I'm saying is to listen to him. See what he has to say. You owe yourself that."

I sniff and nod my head, not believing any of it. There's no doubt that Austin and I have a good friendship. The best. But there's nothing more to it. No matter how much I wish there was.

Chapter 2

Austin

Space. I know she wants space, but I'm not giving it to her. For the last six months, I've tried to be patient and give her a chance to make her own decision. I've had to step up my efforts, and by the way she's glaring at me, she knows what I've done.

"Really?" she asks me.

I shrug, not giving away a thing.

She looks around the salon, and the women under hair dryers have their eyes glued on us. I'm sure that even though they can't hear anything, they are trying to read lips. Ally is sweeping up the hair on the floor from her last client, and I wish she was looking at me instead, but since the moment I walked in here, she's avoided my gaze.

I sit down in the closest vacant chair and wait her out. I know she won't avoid me forever, and I'm willing to wait. That's one advantage to being friends with Ally for so long. I know how she is, and right now, she's overwhelmed, and if it makes her feel better to have time to think things through and form a thought before we talk, I'm fine with it.

After she finishes sweeping, she walks into the back. The ladies sitting under the dryers all look at me, and one peeks her head out. "You going to go after her?"

I look at the door Ally just disappeared through. "No, she'll let me know when she wants to talk to me."

The woman nods her head. "She'll come around. It's those pregnancy hormones. You just have to listen to her and give her what she needs. Every couple argues, but I see you two... you're going to be fine."

I nod, putting way too much value in the words from this woman that I've never talked to before. "Thank you. I appreciate that."

She nods and tucks her head back under the dryer just as Ally comes from the back room. She doesn't look at me, instead staring at the floor in front of me.

I take the opportunity to look at her. Her eyes look tired, and I know she's not resting like she's supposed to be. I'm glad she went out with Natalie and her friends last night, but it looks as if she's paying for it today. I take in the expanse of her belly, and my hands itch at my sides, wanting to touch her. Her long red hair curls down her back, and even now after all these years, she takes my breath away. She's always been beautiful to me, and I hate that she's self-conscious now that she's put on weight. She doesn't realize that she's beautiful this way too.

Ally finally walks over to me after straightening up her station. "Hey, Austin, my schedule is full today. My next appointment should be here any moment. You want me to see if Olivia or someone has an opening?"

I get up from my seat and stand to my full height. "I'm your next appointment."

She looks down at her phone in her hand and then back at me. "You're Kennedy?" She shakes her head and gestures toward her station. "Why did you book it under your middle name?"

I wait until I'm seated before I respond. "Because I thought you would find a way to cancel my appointment or something if you knew it was me. You've been avoiding me."

Her cheeks turn pink, and she looks guilty as she peeks at me in the mirror. "I haven't been avoiding you."

She grabs the apron and lays it over me, securing it at my neck. I keep my gaze fixed on her in the mirror. "You have been, and I'm trying not to take it personally and to give you time..."

She starts to speak, and when she sees the curious gazes from those around us, she leans in, her back to the room, and says what she has to say so low that I have to strain to hear her. "Give me time? You're telling everyone that we're getting married and this is your baby.:."

She puts her hand to her stomach protectively, and I don't fight off the urge any longer. I reach my hand out and cover her hand with my own, curling my fingers around hers. "Ally, I know you hate it when I try to tell you what to do, so I'm going to ask you. Will you please marry me and will you please let me be the father to your baby?"

She gasps and bites on to her lower lip. She wants to say yes, I know she does, but I also know that she's not going to give in so easily. She's already shaking her head. "I can't, Austin. You know I can't."

I hate to be told no, and I don't have to hear it

often, but coming from Ally, it sucks even more. "I know you can. All you have to do is say yes."

She raises up and steps away from my touch. Her hand feathers through my hair, and then she nudges me on the shoulder. "Come on, let's wash it."

She walks away, and I get up to follow her. She's washed my hair every two weeks for the last few years so I know the drill. I get into the chair and lean back. I suck in a breath as she leans over me, her pregnant belly pushed into my shoulder. "I'm not done with this conversation, Ally."

She smiles at me, and it's the first real smile I've seen on her face in a while. "I know you're not. Trust me, I know we'll probably talk this to death, but can we do it somewhere else?"

She lifts her eyes and looks around the room, but my eyes never leave her face. I know what she sees. Everyone is watching us. It's like this everywhere we go, and I know a lot of it has to do with the fact that I've made sure to tell anyone that will listen that Ally and I are getting married. Honestly, it wouldn't be that big of news since we've always been seen together. I'm sure half the town thought we'd end up together anyway. No, the reason they stare is because Ally is still without a ring, and it looks as if she's not going to be giving in any time soon.

"Fine, we can talk about it later. What time do you get off?"

She's washing my hair, and I try to ignore the way her hands feel on me. When she doesn't answer, I ask her again. "What time? I'll bring over dinner."

She's shaking her head again. "Actually, I have plans this afternoon."

She's cagey, looking at everything but me again. "Plans? What kind of plans?"

She shrugs. "Just plans."

I grip the sides of my chair a little tighter. "A date?"

Finally, she looks at me and starts to laugh. I swear she even snorts a little bit. "Really? A date? Have you looked at me lately? No, I don't have a date."

I'm quiet as she finishes washing my hair. I want to ask her more about her plans, but I don't. At one time, we told each other everything, but now she's keeping more and more to herself. It sucks, but lately, I can't seem to reach her.

She finishes rinsing my hair and leans me up to towel it dry. I walk over to her station and take a seat. She goes about combing my hair, and because I can't stop myself, I reach for her hand to hold her in place. Her eyes fix on mine, and I say the thing I've been thinking, the thing I probably shouldn't. Something that I've kept to myself for a long time. "I have looked at you, Ally, and just because you're pregnant, it doesn't make you any less desirable. If anything..." I take a deep breath and let it out slowly. "If anything, you've always been sexy, but seeing you like this just brings out something in a man. So yeah, the idea of you having a date is not outrageous. I just hope if you plan on dating someone, well, I hope it's me."

Her eyes widen, and when I get it all out, her breath is coming out in little pants. She's speechless, and when she continues to just stare at me, it almost feels like a rejection of sorts. I release my hold on her hand but keep my eyes glued on hers. "Austin... I..." She starts and stops, and it's obvious that I've made her uncomfortable. Maybe I'm doing this all wrong. Maybe she doesn't want to tie herself to me.

I force my eyes to the mirror in front of us. "It's okay, Ally. We can talk later."

"But..." she starts, and when she doesn't say anything else, I find her gaze and force a smile to my face. "It's fine, really. I know this isn't the place for us to talk about everything."

She inhales deeply and nods her head. "Right. You're right, of course. So you want the same?"

I know she's talking about my hair, and I nod my

head. She gets to work, and I get lost in thought, thinking of all the things I want. The truth is, I don't want anything to be the same. I wish we could be different. I want more than her friendship. I want the right to touch her, hold her, and tell her that everything's going to be all right. I want to be the one she depends on. I want to be the one she loves. But right now, with the strained silence between us, I'm beginning to wonder if our friendship is going to even make it through this.

Chapter 3

Ally

It's bad.

I can tell by the way the nurse keeps looking up at me as she jots down my numbers. I swear she tsked at me when she saw that I'd gained ten pounds in the last month. Trust me, I don't need her tsking me. I feel the weight of every one of those pounds, and it's punishment enough.

"So?" I ask her after she's taken a urine sample, checked my weight, oxygen, and blood pressure.

She finishes writing, and I'm beginning to wonder if she even heard me when finally, she jumps up from her seat. "Okay, so Dr. Parks is out of town, but Dr. Reynolds is filling in for him. He'll be in soon."

I hold my hands up. "Wait, I want to see Dr. Parks."

The nurse rolls her eyes at me with impatience. "I understand that, but he's out of town. Dr. Reynolds is a great doctor. Plus, he's nice to look at too."

My mouth falls open. Really? Did she really just say that? I'm sure there's some code of ethics or something, and you're not supposed to talk about your doctor being hot with a patient, but obviously Nurse Hatchet doesn't know that. And no, her name is not really Nurse Hatchett, but that's the name I've given her, the one I think she deserves. The last time I was here, she made a big deal about the fact I was pregnant and not married. I thought about switching doctors then, but I couldn't because Dr. Parks has been so wonderful to me. "I don't care if he's nice to look at. I want Dr. Parks." I grab my purse, sling it over my shoulder, and try to make a statement by getting out of my chair, even though it ends up taking me what feels like five tries before I'm finally stable on my feet. "I'll just wait until he's back in town."

I have my hand on the door when she stops me. "Miss Trevers, I don't advise you to leave. Your blood pressure is high, and I suggest you stay to be seen." I pause, but I'm still determined. I love my doctor.

He's an older man that has delivered thousands of babies, and he's nice. I'm about to tell her I'll make another appointment when she continues, "And I understand you want to see Dr. Parks, but for the health of your baby, you should at least stay and let Dr. Reynolds check you out."

I let my head fall. It's not just me anymore. I can't just do what I want; I need to look out for my child now, and even though this baby is a surprise, I already love him or her. I grit my teeth and turn back to my seat. "Fine."

She doesn't gloat or anything since she obviously got her way. She just singsongs, "The doctor will be in shortly" and then walks out the door.

I sit back in my seat and cross my hands over my belly. I'm not sure how long I sit here, but when I wake up, I have a very handsome man with a white coat on standing over me.

"Hi, Miss Trevers, I'm sorry to interrupt your sleep."

I sit up higher in my seat and wipe at my mouth because yes, I even have some drool that has pooled at the corner of my lips. "No, it's fine. I'm sorry for falling asleep."

He pulls his rolling stool over and leans toward me. I will give it to the nurse because she wasn't lying. Dr. Reynolds is nice to look at. He smiles at me. "It's completely understandable. So let's talk."

I nod and cross my hands over my stomach.

He grabs my chart and starts reading before closing it and tilting his head to the side. "You look familiar..."

I push my hair off my face. "Well, I've lived in Whiskey Run my whole life."

He nods. "Aren't you Austin Blaze's..."

Before he can finish that sentence, I tack on. "Best friend? Yes, we've been friends practically our whole lives."

He frowns at that but nods his head. "Right. Well, I've got good news, and I have some bad news. Do you have a preference of what you want first?"

I blow out a breath. "The good news."

He smiles again. "Good. Okay, well the good news is that if you do what I tell you to do, then you and the baby will have a better chance of being healthy."

I can feel a tug in my chest because I know I'm not going to like the bad news. "Well, that is good. So what's the bad news?"

He crosses his arms over his chest. "Uh, do you have someone you'd like to be here with you?"

For the first time since I found out I was

pregnant, real fear takes over. I'm nervous by the change of his tone. I grip the sides of my chair. "Doctor, quite honestly, you're freaking me out. Please tell me what's wrong."

He crosses his arms over his chest and nods. "Okay, well, we found protein in your urine, and your blood pressure is high. Way too high."

I cross my feet at my ankles which even seems to be a feat. "Uh, what does protein in my urine mean?"

He ignores my question, grabbing for my foot and bringing it up, "You have quite a bit of swelling."

I gulp. "Yep."

"Any headaches?"

I'm not one to ever complain, and even being honest with the doctor right now feels like complaining. "Uh, yes, I usually have one every day, but if I sleep or take a pill"—I hold my hand up —"Dr. Parks said it was okay to take them while pregnant."

Dr. Reynolds nods his head. He's got my file open again and is jotting things down. "Okay, so I know this is not what you want to hear."

I throw a hand up. "Just tell me, Doctor, because right now, you have me freaked out a little bit."

He rolls his little stool closer to me, and his voice

drops at least an octave. "You have to rest, Miss Trevers."

I literally let out a breath of relief. Thank God. Okay, I can do this. "Rest, right. I can do that. And if I do, the baby will be okay?"

He shakes his head. "I don't think I'm explaining myself clearly. What do you do for a living?"

My forehead creases, already not liking where this is going. "I'm a hair stylist."

His frown deepens. "So you're on your feet all day?"

I don't want to, but there's no getting around it. I nod. "Yeah."

He grabs a prescription pad and scrawls something across it before ripping it off the pad and handing it to me. "Here you go. Give this to your boss and let them know you're taking the next two weeks off. But just so you know, Miss Trevers, it may be longer. Now, I'm not going to put you on bed rest... yet."

My mouth hits the floor. "Uh, bed rest? I don't need a note. I'm my own boss, I just rent out a space at the salon, and I can't take two weeks—"

He starts to interrupt, and I hold my hand up. "I can't take two OR MORE weeks off. I mean, I know it's important for me and my baby to eat, so yeah, I can't afford to take time off. I can't."

He reaches over and puts a hand on my shoulder. "I understand what you're saying, but for your health—and the baby's—you really have to. I'm worried about preeclampsia, and that can be dangerous for you both. I think you need to go ahead and prepare yourself that the baby may need to come earlier than expected."

I just stare back at him, speechless. Everything he's said is whirling around in my head, and I'm feeling completely overwhelmed.

He seems to sense that and pats me on the shoulder. "It says here the last time you did an ultrasound, we were unable to see the sex of the baby. What do you think if you hop up here and we take a look?"

I nod, still unable to form a sentence. It seems like my whole world is falling down around me.

He holds his hand out to help me up, and when I'm settled on the bed and leaning back, he asks me again. "You sure you don't want anyone here with you..."

His voice trails off, and I shake my head. "Nope, the, uh, father is not involved."

If anything, his frown gets even deeper. "Oh,

okay. So let's see here. Can you pull your pants down a little right under your belly? Now this may be a little cold at first—sorry, the warmer in this room broke." He squirts some cold jelly on my belly and starts pressing around my stomach. I just emptied my bladder, but I'm afraid that if he keeps pressing the way he is, then I'm going to embarrass myself and pee right here on the table.

He turns a screen so both of us can see it and continues moving around on my belly. The sound of my baby's heartbeat fills the room, and I let out an audible sigh. "Good, steady heartbeat," he says.

I bite on to my lower lip and wait for something to appear on the screen. Right now, it looks just like a grainy television feed. The doctor clicks a few buttons, and the screen freezes as he takes pictures. "Do you want to know the sex of the baby?"

"Yes!" I answer way more enthusiastically than I should in the small, quiet room.

He chuckles and then nods his head. "A daughter. You're having a little girl."

I can't help it; tears start rolling down my cheeks. I make promises to myself and even pray to God that I'm going to love and care for my baby. That she will always be loved.

The doctor hands me some tissues, and when I

use them to wipe my face, he gives me more. "Those are for your belly."

I nod, taking them all. Doctor Reynolds goes on to tell me about what I need to be doing, a prescription he's going to send me home with, and for me to call if I need anything. Honestly, after the ultrasound, it all becomes a blur. All I do know is that I have to take care of my baby... no matter what.

Chapter 4

Austin

The distillery is like a well-oiled machine. Every now and then, something breaks or a formula gets messed up, but for the most part, everything goes smoothly. And yeah, there's always something going on with the employees. Someone calls in for a sick kid or an emergency, but for the most part, our employees are exceptional. It doesn't hurt that we pay well.

But today is not one of the smooth days. Today, we're finishing up on our biggest order of the week, two people are out with colds, and one of the chutes broke halfway through the order. We called in the repairman, and now the chute is in working order, and we called in a few people that would have had a day off today. We're finally getting caught up, and we're going to make the deadline, but barely.

When my phone rings, I answer it automatically. "Austin Blaze."

"Hi Austin. This is Brandon Reynolds."

I'm walking through the distillery watching everything to make sure it's all in working order. "What's up, Doc?"

I roomed with Brandon my one and only year of college. He was some kind of prodigy, graduating high school early and was in his fourth year of college when I was in my first. I'm not sure how we ended up rooming together. I'm sure that my father was hoping Brandon's smartness would wear off on me, but it didn't. If anything, I was a bad influence on him. I often joked with him that he owed me for dropping out because if we had stayed rooming together, he would have partied too much and probably wouldn't have made it to medical school. However, after I dropped out, we stayed in touch, but usually at planned dinners or something. Not random phone calls.

The man on the other end of the line is quiet, and I say his name again. "Brandon? You there?"

"Yeah, I'm here. How have you been? How's business?"

My forehead creases because we just got on the phone, and already this is such an odd conversation. "Uh, well, I'm good, and business is good. Did you call to catch up? I'm sort of in the middle of something right now. Can I call you later?"

"Uh, yeah, sure, I was going to tell you about the patient I had today, but sure, we can talk later."

I freeze because I know Brandon. He's a doctor and the type of man that takes the Hippocratic oath seriously. He's not going to talk about his patients to anyone. Unless.... "Who was your patient?"

Instead of answering, he says. "What's going on with you, Austin? You and Ally have been best friends forever. She didn't remember me, but I can't say I blame her. She has a lot going on right now."

"What's going on, Brandon? Is she okay?"

He still doesn't answer me, and it's starting to piss me off. "I heard you were the father. Ally didn't say that, but that's the rumor. Is that true?"

I tell him what I tell anyone else that asks me. "Ally and her baby are mine."

He blows out a breath, and there's anger in his voice. "Okay, so explain things to me. Why would she tell me that she can't afford to take off work? Why did she come in my office today frazzled, sick, overwrought, and tired? Hell, man, she fell asleep in the room waiting five minutes for me. Her blood pressure is so high, I know that unless she makes some big changes, that baby is going to have to come early."

"Fuck!" I scream out loud. Everyone in the plant stops working and looks at me. I ignore them all and walk out of the plant toward the parking lot.

I'm about to tell Brandon thanks for the heads up, but he's not finished yet. "And why, if she's your woman and that's your baby, is she coming to these doctor appointments by herself? Why is she dealing with all this by herself?"

"She's not going to anymore. Look, it's complicated, but I'm about to uncomplicate it. She's going to rest, and from this point forward she's going to be taken care of. Whether she likes it or not."

"Good. Don't go over there yelling at her and making this worse."

I'm shaking my head as I get into my SUV. The truth is, I'm not sure how I'm going to make her listen to me, but I'm going to have to figure it out. "I won't. I promise. Thanks for the heads up, Brandon."

"You're welcome."

I click off the phone and immediately dial Ally's phone number. It rings five times before going to voicemail. I grip onto the steering wheel, and I know I need a plan. First, I call my assistant manager. I never turn things over, choosing to usually do things on my own, but I'm going to start delegating right now. I give him a list of things that I need done and tell him for the next few weeks, I'm going to be out of pocket a little bit. He can call me if he needs anything.

Second, I pull out of the lot and head over to my house. Ally is not going to like this, I know she's not. I can count the times I've been to her house on two of my hands, but there's no other way. She's always been secure in our friendship. At least I thought she was. She knows my parents, my brothers, everyone loves her and would do anything for her, but there's still a part of her that believes she doesn't fit in with us, which is bullshit. There's no part of me that cares about what side of town she lives on, who her parents are, or anything else. She's always been "my person," and the fact that she lives in a trailer park is not going to come between us. I don't have a choice. She doesn't want to come to my house, so I'm going to hers.

I can pack, pick up groceries and dinner, and be at her house in the next hour or two. I know I'm going to have a fight on my hands, but I'm going to do what Brandon suggested. I'm not going to upset her, but I am going to get what I want. And what I want is Ally... and our baby.

Chapter 5

Ally

Knock. Knock. I lay my head back on the cushion and stare up at the plastered ceiling. I ignore the water stains because I know my roof has a few leaks, but there's nothing I can do about it right now. Ignoring the knock, I clench my eyes closed, hoping that whoever it is goes away.

For just a second, I feel the guilt of not answering the door. It's probably my elderly neighbor, and she's probably just wanting to check on me and make sure I'm doing okay, but I just sat down, and I really don't want to get back up.

Knock. Knock. This time it's louder, and just a few seconds go by, and I hear Austin's voice on the other side. "Ally, I know you're in there. Open up."

My head jerks up so fast I get a little dizzy. What

is Austin doing here? He never comes to the trailer park.

I want to ignore him, but I know there's no use. He's not leaving until he talks to me. "I'm coming," I holler.

I set my feet on the floor and then struggle to get up just as Austin knocks again. I get to the door and jerk it open. "Really? Hold your horses, Austin. I'm a lot slower than I used to be, so take a chill. I mean, I know it's a lot to ask for Austin Blaze to have a little patience, but you should try it just once."

For just a second, it looks as if I've hurt his feelings, but he hides it quickly enough. "Hello to you, too. Can I come in?"

He's gesturing to the grocery bags in his arms and to my house, and I pull the door a little to block his view. "Look, now is not a good time. I just got home, and I'm wanting to rest."

He puts his boot out to block me from closing the door. "Nice try. Let me in. I'm not leaving, Ally."

I lean my head back to look him in the face. "What are you even doing here, Austin? You never come to the trailer park."

His jaw tightens. "First of all, you act like I avoid this place, and I don't. You know I don't care where you live, not like you're meaning. And second of all, the reason I never come is because you're not comfortable having me here, but that's all changing right now."

When I don't budge, he lifts the bags in his arms a little higher. "Look, let me put these down in the kitchen. Then I have dinner in the car I need to bring in. Then we can talk, and if you demand I leave, I will."

I blurt out a laugh. "Yeah, right. I know you, Austin Blaze, and you're not going to leave just because I tell you to. Second of all, what kind of dinner do you have in the car?"

He shifts the bags in his arms again, but I don't feel sorry for him because he can easily carry these bags while running a 5K and wouldn't even lose his breath. He's that in shape. He shakes his head side to side and smirks at me. "Really? You don't know what I would bring you to eat?"

I try to hide the excitement on my face, but I know I'm not successful. "Did you bring me a chicken ranch wrap?"

He nods. "With extra pickles on the side."

I groan and open the door, reaching for the bags in his arms. "Here, I'll grab these. You go get my food."

He pulls the bags back. "Really?" he says with a laugh.

I move to the side and gesture for him to come in. I don't know what I was thinking, but I know Austin, and there's no way he's going to let me carry anything. Before I was pregnant, he never let me lift a finger when we hung out together. Since I got pregnant, I'm lucky he lets me walk on my own two feet. I shouldn't be bothered with it, but I am. I can't help but feel guilty because I know it's not his place to take care of me, but every time I try to tell him that, he disagrees with me.

He walks into my small single-wide trailer, and I keep my eyes focused on him. It's either that or I know I'm going to look around at the barely furnished living room, the peeling paint on the kitchen walls, or the cabinet doors that are hanging on their hinges.

He sets the bags down and then comes straight for me. "Have a seat."

His hand goes to my lower back, and he walks with me to the couch. "Austin, what about my food?"

He laughs. "I'm going to get you situated and then I'm going to go get your food."

He helps me onto the couch, and I shift to avoid the broken spring that is poking in my back. He puts a pillow on the coffee table and then picks my feet off the floor and gently lays them on the pillow. "All right, stay put. I'll be right back."

He gets to the door before I am able to collect myself. "I'm not a dog. You can't just give me orders and expect me to do as you say."

He has one hand on the door and stops to look at me. "That's one of the reasons I'm here, Ally. From this point forward, things are going to be different between the two of us. I'm going to go get the food. I'm going to put the groceries away while you eat, and then we're going to talk."

He doesn't wait for me to respond. He walks out the door, letting the screen door slam behind him. He's gone less than a minute and he's walking back in with a familiar bag from Red's Diner. It's big and stuffed with Styrofoam plates, and I know there's more in it than just my wrap. I groan, "Please tell me you didn't bring the cinnamon Blaze cake."

He sets the bag down on the coffee table and starts pulling out food. "I didn't bring the cinnamon Blaze cake. You said you had to quit eating sweets, so I didn't get it. But I did get some fruit, a side salad, and some vegetable soup."

He grabs the first plate with the chicken wrap and sets it easily on my belly. I can't even be offended because for the last month, this is exactly how I've eaten every meal. I take a bite and chew it slowly. Austin is staring at me, and I lick my lips clean. "Uh, are you going to eat?"

He shakes his head. "I had a late lunch. I'm going to put away the groceries while you eat."

He moves everything close to me so I won't have trouble reaching it and then gets up and walks into the kitchen. I take a few bites before I take the time to ask him the question. "So what's up with the food and the groceries? You know I can feed myself, right?"

He nods and keeps putting stuff away. "I know."

When he doesn't say anything else, I eat some more of the wrap, watching him work.

When he gets to the last of it, I force my eyes to the empty plate in front of me. "Want some fruit?"

He's holding the fruit out to me, and I shake my head. "I'm done. I'm stuffed. Thank you, Austin. The wrap really hit the spot."

"You want me to put this in the fridge so you can eat it later?"

I nod and put one hand over my belly as I lean my head back on the couch. "That would be great."

When he finishes putting everything away, he comes to sit next to me. I try not to tense up, but there's no fighting it. Things have never been awkward between us, but I can't help but feel that our relationship has been strained since I got pregnant, and it hasn't helped that I turned him down when he's tried to convince me to marry him.

I pull my shirt down farther over my belly and try not to fidget. "Okay, so are you going to tell me what you're doing here?"

He moves to the middle cushion to sit right next to me. All I can do is watch as he leans forward, undoes the laces on his boots, slides his shoes off, and then props his feet up on the coffee table next to mine. "I'm staying."

I laugh because I think he's joking, but when all he does is stare at me with that challenging look that he's mastered the last six months, the smile drops from my face. "You're not staying here."

He doesn't react. He just keeps staring at me with that knowing look on his face.

"Austin, you're not staying here."

He just laughs. "I am. I packed a bag. It's in my SUV, but I'll get it out in a minute. Do you want to watch some TV?"

He picks up the remote, and I pull it from his hands. "Austin, you're not staying here."

He nods. "Yes, I am."

I sputter. "But why?"

He drops his feet to the floor and turns toward me as he puts a hand on my knee. "Because I'm going to take care of you."

I cut him off. "I can take care of myself."

I don't know if it's the stress of the day or what, but emotions hit me hard. I'm wiping at the tears on my face as fast as they fall. I'm sobbing, and Austin probably can't even make out what I'm saying, but I can't stop rambling. "Why does no one think I can take care of myself? I'm doing the best that I can. I know I need to do better, and I'm trying. I'm trying so hard, Austin, but it's not good enough. I'm not good enough... hell, I can't even keep my baby healthy... myself healthy—"

He pulls me into his lap and circles his arms around me. I don't fight him, and I lay my head on his shoulder and let my body melt into his. He kisses the top of my head. "Fuck, please stop crying, Ally. I can handle anything but when you cry, you know that."

But if anything, I cry harder. He's rubbing my back with big strokes of his hands. "I'm sorry," I sob.

He squeezes me tighter. "No. Don't say that. You never have to apologize to me. Come on, Ally. We're going to take this one day at a time. You're my best friend in the whole world. You know me better than anyone, and you know that if I didn't want to do something, I wouldn't do it. I want to do this. I want to take care of you. I want to take care of our baby."

"Girl," I mutter. "I found out today I'm having a girl."

He gasps. "A daughter? That's amazing, baby. You're going to be the best mom. And I'm going to probably end up in jail the first time some boy asks her out, but we'll figure it out.... Are you happy, Ally?"

I shrug my shoulders and turn my head to bury my face in his neck. My hands grip at his waist, and I burrow into him. "Yeah, I'm happy, but I'm scared, Austin. I'm so scared."

I can feel him take a deep breath and let it out slowly. "I'm here for you, Ally. Always. You just have to let me in and let me be here for you." He leans back on the couch but doesn't let go of me. "Rest, baby. I know you're tired. Let me hold you."

I can't resist him because for the first time in a long time, it's nice to just let my troubles melt away and to have someone else bear the brunt of it all. I let my eyes close, and the last thing I remember thinking before I fall asleep is that I could get used to this.

Chapter 6

Austin

I lean back in my chair, and to my brothers, I probably look calm, cool, and collected. I've tried to stay alert through the whole meeting, even when Beau went on and on about spreadsheets, but the longer I sit here, the more antsy I get. I haven't heard from Ally all morning, and as soon as this meeting is over, I'm going to hightail it out of here and check on her.

Last night, sleeping on the couch with her in my arms gave me just a glimpse of what our future could look like, and there's no way I'm giving up on it now.

Lost in thought, I jerk when Ford calls my name. I look up, and all four of my brothers are staring at me expectantly. I lean forward and put my arms on the table in front of me. My leg is bouncing under the table, but otherwise, I try to appear calm. "Right, my turn. Sorry. Yeah, the distillery is going well. I've had my assistant stepping in to help some more, but the orders are all going well, and we're on top of everything. I had to have a chute repaired yesterday so I ordered another one. We'll install the new one and use the repaired one as a backup. Other than that, everything's good."

Ford nods his head. "Okay, sounds good."

I tap my fist on the top of the table twice, force a smile to my face, and get up. "So we good? Same time, next week?"

"Austin, what's going on?" My brother Huddy asks. I look at him and my other brothers, and they all have worried looks on their faces. I can't really blame them. I know I haven't been the same lately, and they've given me some space to try and work things out, but I knew it wouldn't last forever.

"Nothing's going on. I'm sorry, I thought we were done, but if not, I'm good. What's left to talk about?" I turn to my brother who's the CFO and loves to talk about data, ROI, and all that shit. "Beau, you got another spreadsheet you want to go over?"

Huddy barely holds back a laugh. "Look, you're our baby bro. We're just worried about you, that's all."

I hook my thumb toward Lucas. "He's the baby of the family. Worry about him."

Huddy leans toward me and clasps his hand on my shoulder. "Talk to us, Austin. What's going on? How's Ally?"

I shake my head and run my fingers across my temples. "Her blood pressure is high. Too high, and the doctors want her to rest, but of course she won't. She promised she'd slow down, and she's trying but..." I break off in frustration.

"But what?" Lucas asks.

I shake my head, knowing the irony of what I'm about to say. "She says she doesn't have the money to take off from her job."

"Fuck, Austin—"

I hold my hand up before Huddy can finish his thought. "Yes, I've tried to offer her money. I've tried to tell her not to worry about anything, but she's so damn independent, she thinks she can do it all without help. I'm practically forcing her to depend on me, and I'm not sure if that's the right thing to do or not, but I can't just stand by and let her hurt herself or her baby."

Huddy's hand on my shoulder tightens, and my other brothers get out of their chairs and circle around the conference table to come toward me. Beau is the first to ask, "What can we do, Austin?"

I shrug, not knowing what to tell them. "I moved in with her."

"At the trailer park?"

My eyes flare at Ford. "Don't be a snob."

He rolls his eyes. "I'm not. What can we do? There has to be something."

"Nothing. There's nothing anyone can do. It's ultimately up to her to rest. It's not like I can force her to quit her job or to sit down and prop her feet up."

Lucas leans against the table. "I don't understand. We all love Ally. Hell, she's been a part of our family since you were in middle school. I know she's your best friend, but she's always been like a little sister to us. We can't just stand by and do nothing."

I throw my hands up in the air. "I know that."

Ford crosses his arms over his chest. "I don't understand. You love her."

I don't even attempt to deny it. I do love Ally and as more than just a friend.

And then Ford looks at me pointedly. "And she loves you, too."

"She doesn't love me." I say it with force, but even I can hear the hope in my voice.

Ford plants his feet and tilts his head. "Okay, if you believe that, then what are you doing? You've told everyone that will listen that you're marrying her and she's having your baby. If you believe that, believe that she doesn't love you, then what are you doing?"

I ram my hand through my hair and shake my head. "You don't understand."

Huddy interrupts. "Then explain it to us."

"I thought I could let her be with someone. I thought I could stand by and let her have her family with someone else. I want her to be happy and to have everything she wants, but I can't let her go. I fuckin' can't let her go."

Beau's bellow surprises us all. "Then don't! Don't let her go!"

All of us turn to him. He's the most mild mannered of all of us, and this kind of reaction from him has my jaw dropping. He doesn't notice or seem to care. "Fuck, Austin. We've all seen you together. You love each other. Everyone knows it... you know it. She probably feels like you've had this change of heart because you're feeling sorry for her or some shit. She doesn't realize you've been a coward all these years. She doesn't realize you've always been in love with her and have kept your relationship platonic because you're a pussy."

Ford steps between Beau and me and puts his hands up between us. "That's enough, Beau. Look, Austin. Whatever you need from us, whatever Ally needs from us, we're here. You can fix this, brother." He wraps his hand around the back of my neck. "Trust me, do whatever you have to do to fix this because the end result is worth it. Love is worth it."

I want to be mad. They've cussed me and called me names, but I've deserved every one of them. I deserve all of this. "I know. Fuck, I know it's worth it. She's worth it. I need to go. I need to check on the shipments going out today before I go home. And I need to check on Ally."

Each of my brothers takes a turn hugging me before I walk out. They're the only ones that can cuss me one second and hug me the next, but I wouldn't trade one of them for anything.

And I know they're right. I can't fuck this up. I need to fix it because I know that Ally and I are meant to be together. It may have taken me awhile to get my shit together, but I can see how good we can be together. I just have to convince her to give me a chance... and then make sure she never regrets it.

Chapter 7

Ally

It's after work, and I'm exhausted. I feel as if I can barely lift my head off the couch. Austin cooked dinner, plying me with protein and vegetables. He's waited on me hand and foot, refusing my offer to clean up since he cooked, and insisted I sit here and rest. I should be in a good mood. My blood pressure is in the normal range, I've been fed, and I have nothing to do until I have to be at work tomorrow, but I can't seem to get myself out of this funk.

I'm sure it has nothing to do with the fact that Austin is walking around my house without his shirt on. Has he always looked this good? I wave my hand in front of my face because it feels like it's gotten at least ten degrees hotter in here in the last few minutes.

Why is it so sexy to watch him load the dishwasher? The muscles in his back flex as he moves, and I bite my lip to hold in the groan. He closes the door to the dishwasher, and I force my eyes to the popcorn ceiling.

As he walks into the living room, I keep my eyes averted. Austin knows me better than anyone, and I definitely don't want him figuring out what I'm thinking right now.

He stands next to the couch, and I still focus on the ceiling as if I'm enthralled by the water stain that's been there as long as I can remember.

"What's wrong, Ally?"

"Nothing," I mutter.

"Ally." He sing-songs my name, and I force myself to look at him.

"What?"

He's standing over me with his hands on his hips. Damn, he's handsome. He's making me feel things that I haven't felt in a long time.

"Talk to me. What's wrong?"

I close my eyes because he's too much to look at. That's it. For the next few months until these pregnancy hormones are under control, I'm going to just refrain from looking at him. "Nothing's wrong."

He leans toward me and brushes the hair off my face. "Talk to me, Ally. Something's bothering you."

When I ignore him, he asks again. "Ally..."

With my eyes closed, I ask him, "Do you know, everyone in town thinks we're getting married?"

"Yep," he answers.

I clench my eyes shut. "And that everyone thinks this baby is yours?"

He's just as fast to answer. Absolutely no hesitation. "Yep."

I let out a long breath. "We're not getting married, Austin."

He just laughs. "Yes, we are."

"No, we're not."

I shrug my shoulder, refusing to fight with him about this. I feel his leg brush my arm, and I assume he's walking away. I'm surprised when I feel him wrap his hands around my ankles. My eyes fly open, and I come up on my elbows. "What are you doing?"

He lifts my legs and sits down, then rests my feet on his lap. "Relax, I'm just going to massage your feet, that's all."

I'm about to protest until he presses his fingers

into the arch of my foot, and instead of stopping him, I let my head fall back with a loud, guttural groan.

He stops, and I jerk my head up to look at him. "God, don't stop."

He chuckles and grips my foot. "I'm not." He presses into my feet, moving from one to the other. I can't stop the sounds that fall from my lips, and I don't even try. Whatever he's doing to me, it feels good.

He moves his hands up my calf and massages me there. "Fuck, Austin, that feels good."

I can't resist now. I open my eyes and watch him as his hands move up and down my legs. He's smiling as he soothes my sore muscles.

His touch goes deeper, and I moan again. "Seriously, if this whole whiskey thing doesn't pan out, then you could definitely get a job as a masseuse."

"Ha! Good to know, but I don't plan on going around giving around massages to people I don't know."

I roll my eyes and try to act like the thought of him giving massages to someone else doesn't bother me when in fact, it drives me crazy. I instantly see red. Just the thought of him touching another woman has me tensing up.

He pats my leg. "What's up? You're supposed to be relaxing. Why are you tensed up? What's going on in that pretty head of yours?"

"Nothing."

He pats my leg again and starts on the other one. I stretch my feet out and gasp as I feel it nudge against something hard and erect. I freeze. I should pull away and act like nothing happened, but that's not who I am. I flex my foot again, and it's still there. I'm not imagining it. "Uh, Austin?"

He adjusts my feet away from his bulge. His voice is low and strained. "Yeah, baby?"

I swear there's a tug in my lower belly when he calls me baby. "Uh, what do you have going on down there?"

"If you're going to moan like that, I'm going to react."

I throw one arm over my eyes. "Good to know it only takes a sound."

He stops massaging my feet and wraps both his hands around my ankles. "I'm not a pervert. It takes more than a sound."

I grit my teeth. "Well, good thing you can go take care of it."

I don't want to think about him with another

woman, and the idea that he may leave here and go to some woman to satisfy himself makes me ill.

His hands tighten on my ankles. "Ally..."

"What?" I ask him, unable to hide my anger.

"You sound mad."

I soften my voice, even though my hands are still formed into fists. "I'm not mad. I mean, there's no reason one of us shouldn't be scratching their itch. Live it up, Austin. Have fun."

He trails his thumbs in circles over my ankles, and I'm doing my best to not let my body react. He starts to stroke his finger up and down. "Soooooo, you think that I'm going to what? Go out, find some random woman to take care of my hard cock?"

I gasp and lift my arm from my eyes so I can see him. I can't believe he just said that. Austin and I are close, but he's never talked to me about stuff like this. My surprise doesn't stop him, though. He continues, "I mean, that doesn't seem fair, right? You're the reason I'm in this condition. You're the reason that I'm about to come in my shorts... and you think I should go and let some other woman take care of it?"

I lift my foot to kick at his leg. "Funny, Austin. You know I didn't cause that."

He shifts in his seat and sits up a little higher. "Trust me, Ally. You're the only reason I'm like this."

He drops that bombshell, and all I can do is stare at him, open-mouthed, in shock. Is he being for real right now? How long have I wished for something more with Austin? Only more than half my life. After high school, I knew I had no hope. He had girlfriend after girlfriend, and there was no way I could compare. I gave up any hope of thinking there could be something between us. I accepted that we would never be anything more than friends. So why is he acting like this?

Chapter 8

Austin

"You're just horny, Austin. You've been too busy trying to take care of your pregnant best friend instead of taking care of"—she points at my nether regions—"that. You need to go get laid."

I stare at her, and I'm completely conflicted. I've always played it safe with her. Never have I ever allowed myself to flirt with her or say anything inappropriate, even though I've definitely had those thoughts. I shrug as I come to the conclusion that I'm done holding back. If I want Ally, I'm going to have to let her know I do. "I am horny. I haven't had sex in a few years."

It's a bombshell for her. I know it is. She thinks I have some kind of active sex life, but the truth is, I don't. She struggles on the couch, but I reach for her hand and pull her up as she practically shouts at me, "Do what? A few years? You're lying."

I fix her with a glare. "Right, because I always lie to you."

She starts to stutter and shakes her head. "Shit, you're serious."

I know it's more of a rhetorical question, but I still nod my head. "Yep. I'm serious."

Her mouth is hanging open. "But why? It doesn't make sense. Women throw themselves at you."

I roll my eyes at her. "I don't just sleep with anyone that shows interest in me."

She nods. "I know that, but that still doesn't explain how you haven't had sex in... years."

I lift one leg on the couch and turn to face her. She's sitting the same way, and our legs are touching. "Are you sure you want to know?"

She looks at me worriedly for a second. "Oh my God, Austin." She puts her hand to her mouth and whispers, "Do you have something?"

I rear back in surprise. "What? No, of course not. Geez, if you want to know it all, I've slept with three women, and I've wrapped it up every time."

She pushes her hand against my chest. "Bullshit, Austin. There's no way you've only slept with three women. We're in our thirties."

I take a deep breath and let it out. "The first was in college and uh, I was stupid. It meant nothing. The second one was—"

She cuts me off, holding up her hand with a disgusted look on her face. "I don't want to hear about women you've slept with."

I nod, understanding. Every time I think of her with the baby's father, I want to punch something. "I get it. I don't want to talk about men you've slept with."

She nods and then tilts her head. "Okay, I have to ask. Why? Why haven't you slept with a woman in so long?"

I rub my hand which is sweaty down the thighs of my shorts. "I'm not talking about this with you."

She laughs. "Oh hell no, you can't drop a bombshell like that and then not tell me the story. Why have you not—"

I don't want to hear her say *sex* again because it puts all kinds of images in my head. "Because I can't... you know..."

She curls her nose up. "You can't.... What... get it up?" If that's not bad enough, she points her finger out straight and then makes it limp.

I grab on to her hand. "Yeah, that about sums it up."

She's shaking her head before I even finish and starts to laugh. "But that's not true... it works... I felt it. I mean, I felt it against my foot. You can definitely get hard."

I don't let go, but I do let our hands fall onto my leg between us. "You're right, Ally. I can definitely get hard... with you."

She points at herself as her eyes widen. "With me?"

I can't help but laugh. Does she really not have any idea? "Yes, when I think of you, when I see you, when I touch you... I'm hard."

She pulls away from my hand and tries to scoot back, but I grab on to her waist to hold her still. "Where do you think you're going? You wanted to talk about this, and you're right. It's past time. I think we need to talk about this. It's about time we got it out in the open, don't you think?"

She sounds as if she's about to burst into tears. "You're lying to me, Austin."

I deny it instantly. "I'm not lying to you."

She crosses her arms over her ample chest. Her red hair is wild around her head, her lips are puckered, and her eyes are wet. "I don't need you to feel sorry for me."

"Feel sorry for you?" I burst out. "I don't feel sorry for you. What are you talking about?"

She points at her belly and then waves it up and down her body. "So I'm supposed to believe that you're attracted to all this?"

"Yes, because I am."

She tilts her head to the side and searches my face. "Do you have some kind of pregnancy fetish or something? Because before this you never looked at me twice."

"I couldn't... I wouldn't let myself." I try to explain, but I know I'm not doing a good job of it.

She takes a deep breath and blows it out slowly. "I can't do this right now. I'm not thinking right. I have all these stupid hormones going crazy inside me. I'm thinking things—wanting things—I shouldn't be wanting. And you know what, you walking around here half naked is not helping matters. Forget it, Austin. We don't need to do this. I'm not sure what we're doing, but I don't need you to fix all my problems for me."

I scoot closer to her, wrapping my hands around her elbows to hold her in place. "What if I want to take care of your problems? This one, especially?"

She's searching my eyes. I see the fear in hers, and I know it's the same look reflected in mine. I wouldn't be honest if I didn't say a part of me is scared. Of course I'm worried about changing our friendship. I want things to be the same... but I want more.

I bring my hands up and brush her hair back, tucking it behind her ears. "Lie back, Ally."

She trembles and bites onto her lower lip. Her eyes are dilated, and I know she's feeling everything I'm feeling right now. I knew being close to her, living under the same roof would be a test for me, and I've never been happier to fail a test in my life. When she doesn't move, I tell her again as I gently push her backwards, "Lie down, Ally."

She goes to her back, and I lay her feet on my lap. I don't even try to keep her away from my hard manhood. "But..." she starts.

I shake my head slowly. "No buts. Just let me do this for you."

She rubs her hand across her swollen belly. "What exactly are you going to do for me?"

I don't hesitate. "Make you feel good... maybe relieve a little bit of stress for you."

She looks at me, and I see the desire flare on her face. She wants this, but I don't trust she's going to just give in. I know she's scared. Hell, I'm scared, but

I'm even more scared about losing her. "Do you trust me, Ally?"

She rolls her eyes. "You know I do."

I nod and let my eyes rove up her body. From where I'm sitting, with her feet in my lap, I have a perfect view. Now if she wasn't so tense, I could take full advantage of this situation. "Okay, so." I should feel bad about it, but I don't. I cup my hard manhood in my shorts and give it a healthy tug before wrapping my hand back around her foot. "Since you trust me, I need you to let me do something."

I try to stop her from tensing up by massaging her feet and then up and over her ankles. She's restless as she stretches out her legs, but I don't stop my movements. Her voice is husky when she finally asks me the question. "What do you want me to let you do?"

I smile because all the images are in my head. Her in bed curled against my body. Her riding me, grinding herself on my cock. I want all of it, but I know I need to take it slowly. "I just want to make you feel good."

She's interested. It's obvious by the way her eyes light up. "That's it? You just want to make me feel good? What about you?"

Although I appreciate her concern, all it does is

tell me that she really has no idea. "Trust me, making you feel good is going to make me feel good."

She nudges her foot against my cock, and I grunt as I grab it. I groan as she laughs. "You sure about that?"

"Yep." I slap her thigh and then tug on her shorts. "Take these off."

Her eyes about bulge out of her head. "You want me to take my shorts off?"

She's stalling, and I'm tired of waiting. "Lie back and close your eyes."

She looks at me with insecurity in her eyes. "Austin... I'm too—" She huffs and waves her hand across her body. "You don't want to see all this."

"Oh, I do."

She's trying to pull away, but I know it's only because she's self-conscious. I grab the edges of her shorts and pull them down. "Lift up."

She lifts up a little, and I pull her shorts down her legs. The scrap of material between her thighs is a darker shade than the rest of the material, telling me that she's already wet for this. I can't resist. I put my finger on the sodden material. "You want this, Ally? You want me to make you feel good?"

She lifts her hips just a bit and presses into my

hand. "I do, Austin, but not at the expense of it messing up us. I can't lose you... not now."

I run my finger along the silky material covering her slit. "You'll never lose me... and nothing is going to mess this up between us."

Finally, she nods, and I let out my breath in a whoosh. As if I'm afraid she's going to change her mind, I reach for each side of her panties and hook my fingers in the waistband before tugging them down. She lifts her hips enough for me to get the material down her hips and I pull them off her feet.

She snaps her knees together, blocking me from seeing her. I lean forward and kiss her kneecap and then lean my chin there. "You know that you holding your knees together is not going to stop me, right?"

She looks at me with a challenge in her eyes. "If I told you no, I don't want this, you'd stop, Austin."

I have both hands on her knees now, ready to part her legs, but I freeze at her words. "You don't mean that. You want this, Ally. You want me to make you feel good."

The blank expression on her face worries me, but I know I'm right. I know she wants this. "Are you going to let me touch you?"

I hold my breath, waiting for her to respond. She's right. If she says she doesn't want this, I'd stop, no matter how much it would hurt to do it. When she doesn't respond, I lean my bare chest against her legs and loop my arms around her bent knees. "Be honest with yourself, be honest with me. You want me... you need me to touch you, Ally. All that matters right now is me and you and what we want. I want to touch you, to taste you. That's what I want. But I need to know what you're thinking. What about you? Tell me what you want."

She inhales deeply, and I'm completely on edge as I wait for her response. It's only when I feel her legs start to fall open that I loosen my grip on her. She leans her head back on the couch. "You. I want you to make me feel good, Austin. I want to forget about everything for just a few minutes."

I scoot to the edge of the couch, lifting her foot and putting it behind me so I'm sitting between her legs. The abrupt change in positions has her breaths coming in pants. Her legs are open, and I have a perfect view of her. I must sit here too long because her hands go down her belly, and she tries to cover herself from me.

I stop her, though, grabbing both her hands and putting them above her belly. "All I need you to do is lean back and enjoy. Don't get all up in your head Don't worry about what I may be thinking—"

She laughs, and a snort comes out, causing me to smile. "Right. I can't relax. Not with you staring at me like—"

It's my turn to cut her off. "What? Staring at you like I haven't eaten in days? Like I have the prettiest woman laid out, open for me and I get to feast on her? Because that's how I'm staring at you."

I can't keep my hands off her. I let my hands push her thighs open, and I stroke up and down her soft skin. She's practically vibrating under my touch. I stroke my fingers through her swollen slit, and she practically leaps off the couch. I press my arm over her hips, careful to not smash the baby. When I touch her again, I press my finger to her swollen nub, circling it with more pressure at each pass around. She tenses but not from insecurity or trying to hide from me. Nope, she's already so close it won't take long for her to come undone.

She's all primed and pink. I'm relentless as I focus on giving her exactly what she needs as her hips slowly gyrate up and down. Her arousal is coating my finger. She's obviously feeling good, and I know I can make her come like this, but my next move is completely selfish. I kiss her knee again. "Ally, look at me."

She looks at me through hooded eyes. She's so close already. "Yeah, Austin?"

"I want to taste you."

Her eyes widen. "You don't have to... do that."

"I want to. I really, really want to. Can I put my mouth on you?"

She's affected by my question, and I swear she soaks my finger. I groan as it slides through her silky folds. "I want to taste you, Ally."

She nods her head, and I kiss her knee before moving down her inner thigh. I scoot to the floor, putting her legs over my shoulders. I inhale, letting her sweet scent fill my nostrils. When I finally reach the v of her legs, I can't stop. I press my tongue to her, swiping through her slit. I kiss and lick her until she's moaning my name over and over. Her hand is wrapped around the back of my neck, and I can feel her nails dig into my skin, but I don't stop. When I wrap my lips around her clit, she comes undone, but I don't stop. I need to make sure she has no doubt how much I can please her. I need her to want more of this... of us.

Chapter 9

Ally

My whole body is pulled taut. Right now, I can't even try to form a coherent sentence. All I can do is try to regulate my breathing and come down off my high. It shouldn't have felt that good. Austin is my best friend. We've never crossed the line like this, and I wait for the doubt and insecurity to take over, but it doesn't. It's impossible to feel anything except good right now.

Austin raises up, and all I can do is stare at him. HIs mouth is covered with my arousal, and he's licking his lips. The look he's giving me causes a tug in my lower belly. I start to stutter. "Soooo, uh, you, uh?"

He licks his lips again and then wipes his mouth

with his hand before sucking off his finger... the one that was inside me. "You okay? The baby okay?"

I nod, covering my belly with my hand. "I'm okay... I'm good. Actually, I'm really good."

"Really good, huh? I was hoping for excellent, extremely satisfied, or something else along those lines." He levels me with a look. "It's okay, something to look forward to for next time."

I sit up, and I shouldn't have because it brings me even closer to Austin, and being this close to him is already messing with me. "I'm extremely satisfied, and there's not going to be a—"

He cuts me off before I can tell him there won't be a next time. He turns so I can see the back of his neck. "See that?"

He points at the red marks across his neck, and I reach for him. "Did I do that?"

He grabs my hand and holds it between us. "Yep, you did that. I know it was more than good, Ally and yes, there will definitely be a next time. Once is not enough."

We're close, too close. I can see the fire in his eyes and feel his chest expand against my arm with every breath he takes. I'm about to argue with him and tell him all the reasons why this is a bad idea, but I don't have it in me right now. I pull my hand from him and sit back. "Thank you. I mean, for uh, what you did. Thank you."

He shakes his head. "You don't have to thank me for that. I wanted to do it."

I nod. "Right. Well, it doesn't change anything, Austin."

He just smiles at me with a knowing smirk. "It changes everything. Do you really think that I'll be okay with just eating you one time? Like I said, one taste is not enough."

I reach my hand out to smack his chest as heat rushes through my body. I'm trying to keep my cool, but it's almost impossible. I'm sitting here, naked from the waist down and trying to convince myself that this was a one-time thing. "We're friends, Austin." I point to my shorts on the floor. "Can you hand me my panties and my shorts?"

He picks them up off the floor but doesn't hand them to me. He leans down and puts my feet into the legs of my underwear. As he helps me get my shorts to my ankles, he answers me. "Yes, we are friends."

"I'm pregnant."

He leans forward and kisses my belly. My heart does a somersault in my chest at the same time he says, "I know you're pregnant."

Holding my breath, I tell him, "With another man's baby."

He helps me stand up and then pulls my underwear and shorts up my hips. "SHE is our baby, Ally. Nothing you can say is going to convince me otherwise."

I shake my head, feeling overwhelmed. "Austin..."

He takes a step toward me, and our faces are mere inches apart. I suck in a breath, wondering if he's going to kiss me. All I'd have to do is lean in just a little, and our lips could touch. He's staring at my mouth. "You said it yourself, baby. You said the donor doesn't want a relationship with the baby."

I nod because I've already come to terms with all this. I want to laugh because that's what Austin has called the father since I've told him about the baby. He's called him the donor. "I know, but that doesn't mean—"

He cuts me off, "You and our baby are mine. The sooner you get on board with this, the sooner we can get on with our lives."

He doesn't realize how long I've waited to hear this from him. For years, I've wished there was something more than friendship between us, but I wasn't holding out hope. He never gave me any indication that he felt anything more for me. No one can blame me for wondering if this is just a pity thing on his part. "Austin," I start, but I stop when a high-pitched car alarm goes off outside. I'm about to step around Austin when he stops me with his hands to my shoulders. "Where do you think you're going?"

I try to move around him, but he stops me. "Austin, I'm sure that's probably your car alarm. I'm going to go—"

He blocks my path. "You're going to sit right here. Listen to me, I can't be worrying about you and the baby. Stay here. Call Huddy; he lives the closest. I'll be right back."

He turns to go, and I know he must doubt that I'll listen because he turns back to me. "Stay here. Think about the baby."

I put a protective hand over my belly and nod my head, even though letting him go out into the dark is the last thing I want to do. He locks the door before he shuts it behind him. As soon as he's gone, I jump into action.

I grab my phone and dial Huddy. "Someone's breaking into Austin's car, and he went out into the dark by himself. He told me to call you."

"Where? Where are you?"

Shit. Right, that information would be helpful.

"My house."

"I'm on my way. Stay inside, Ally."

As soon as he gives me the order, I hear the phone click. I put down the phone and am staring outside. Even with the floodlights, it's hard to see what's happening. Until I see them at the corner of the driveway. I count the number of people, and when I get to three and know Austin is outnumbered, I know I can't just stay in here and watch.

Opening my closet by the front door, I grab the baseball bat and then tiptoe out the back door. I get around the corner, and sure enough, there are two of them against Austin. One is holding him as the other one is punching him. I don't think twice. I pull the bat back and then swing it as hard as I can at the guy hitting Austin. I hit him in the back, and he goes sprawling across the gravel with a groan.

The guy holding Austin lets go of him and comes for me. I run around to the other side of Austin's car. The man is following me, but right when he reaches for me, he's pulled backward as Austin bellows, "Don't fuckin' touch her."

They fight, and the sound of fists pounding into flesh has me feeling queasy. I can't see anything from where I'm standing, but I'm too scared to move.

When the hitting stops, I can't stand it any longer. "Austin. Austin, please tell me you're okay."

He comes around the car, bent over, holding his ribs. I rush over to him. "Austin, oh my God, are you okay?"

His voice is strangled. "I told you to stay inside."

Filled with worry and indignation, I tell him, "I wasn't going to stay inside and let them kill you."

He pulls me against his chest. "If anything happened to you, I might as well be dead."

I'm trying to analyze that thought when a truck comes to a screeching halt in the road in front of my house. Austin puts me behind him, ready to defend me against the unknown when Huddy comes into the light. "Fuck, Austin. You okay?"

Before he can answer, more cars pull into the trailer park, and the last one has red and blue lights flashing on top.

Austin never lets go of me. He talks to the police and his brother with one arm around me. All the neighbors are outside, trying to see what's going on. The police pick the guys up off the ground and put them both in the back of the squad car. It's not until they're gone that exhaustion seems to take over. I'm leaning into Austin as we walk up the steps to my house.

Huddy and Austin seem to have some unspoken words because I hear Huddy say, "I'll be right here" as he sits on my front porch when Austin leads me inside.

I point my thumb outside. "What's he going to do? Sit out there all night?"

Austin pulls me to a stop in my living room. He puts his hands on each side of my face. He's mad. I've known him long enough to know that right now, he's barely containing his anger. "You could have been hurt. Our baby could have been hurt."

I put my hands up to break the hold he has on me, but he doesn't budge, so instead I hold on to his arms. "Austin, I couldn't just stay in here and let them kill you."

He's shaking his head. "I don't care about me. You're all that matters."

"You matter to me, and I know you're mad, but I couldn't stay in here. I couldn't just let them hurt you." I let out a sob and try to keep from crying, but I can't. "You can be mad at me all you want, but I'm not ever going to just stand by and let people hurt you."

His eyes widen, and he shakes his head before pulling me against his chest in a tight hug. "I swear, you drive me crazy, woman."

I try not to let his words hurt me. My arms go around him, and he's still shirtless. I hold on to him, trying not to squeeze too hard because I know he's hurt. "Maybe you should go home, Austin. Maybe it's for the best. Tonight has been crazy, to say the least."

He nods. "Oh, I'm going home, but I'm taking you with me."

I gasp and step back from him. "I'm not going with you."

He laughs. "Ally, I wasn't asking you. You're going with me. Those were drug dealers. They were hopped up on something, and we're not staying here to see what they or their buddies plan to do next."

I want to argue with him, but I know he's right. The neighborhood used to be filled with working class families just trying to make a living. In recent years, it's gone downhill fast. Drugs and prostitution are problems here now. I always try to keep to myself, but I knew the day would come when I would get their attention. Of course the shiny SUV in my driveway drew them in.

There's a slight twinge in my belly, and the feeling catches me by surprise. Instinctively, my hand goes to my belly, and I feel it again.

"Are you okay, Ally?"

Chapter 10

Austin

When she doesn't answer me, I cover her hand with my own. "Ally, are you okay? Talk to me."

She takes in a breath. "Yes, um, I'm fine."

"Sit."

When she doesn't move, I lean over and lift her up in my arms and make my way to the couch. "Sit. I'm going to pack you a bag."

She shakes her head. "Austin—"

I can't take it any longer. I lean in and press my lips to hers. I kiss her until we're both breathless. We've never kissed, not like this, and as soon as our lips meet, it's addicting. I wrap my hand around the back of her head and hold her to me. Her lips open, and I take full advantage by swiping my tongue next to hers. She whimpers, and I pull back, searching her eyes. She's looking at me curiously, and I know we have a lot to talk about, but now is not the time. I need to get her out of here, but I'm not moving until she understands a few things. We're both breathless. I cup her cheeks and look into her eyes. "Will you do this for me, please? I need you with me, Ally. Will you please go with me?"

She's stunned, and she's blinking at me with her wide eyes. "Okay."

She barely gets the words out and I kiss her again, just a peck this time, and then I'm off to her bedroom. I grab her clothes out of the closet and sling them over my arm. I go to the front porch and stop next to Huddy. "Can you put these in my car?"

He takes them from my arms. "I'm going to swap cars with you for the night. There's glass all in yours. I'll get it cleaned up tomorrow and then we can swap back."

I nod. "Thanks, Huddy. And thanks for coming so quick."

He nods with a grunt. He's mellowed some since he got with Elle, but he still has trouble processing emotions sometimes. "Sure, no problem, brother."

He steps off the porch, and I go back inside. Trip after trip, I carry Ally's stuff outside. I wait for her to object or try to stop me, but every time I walk past her, she's staring at me with her fingers pressed to her still swollen lips.

After I've cleared out her drawers and the bathroom, I go back in for her as I'm pulling on a T-shirt. I pull out my phone, shoot off a text to the doctor, and then help Ally up from the couch. "You ready?"

She nods, visibly shaken now. "Yeah, I'll just stay a few days, Austin. Just enough for things to die down and then I'll come back home."

I'm nodding my head as I lead her out the door. She must not have been paying attention because I packed all her clothes. Huddy's waiting for us, and I lead Ally over to his truck. "My window's broken, and Huddy's letting us use his truck so you don't sit on broken glass or anything."

She sighs worriedly. "Your whole family is going to hate me before this is over with."

Huddy opens the passenger door to his truck. "Nope, no chance. His whole family already loves you. I'm pretty sure most of us would pick you over Austin anyway."

Ally laughs, and I let it flow over me. I've always loved the sound of her laugh, but right now, I need to hear it.

When I've thanked Huddy again and we're pulling out of the neighborhood, I break it to Ally. "We're going to see your doctor."

Ally turns in her seat. "It's late. I'll go tomorrow to make sure everything is okay."

The fact that she's not telling me straight-out no worries me even more. "I already called, and he's meeting us there."

She puts her hand on the dashboard, and I realize I'm driving too fast. I take my foot off the pedal as she tells me, "My doctor is out of town."

I don't respond. I'm not sure how to respond, so instead, I change the subject. "How are you feeling?"

"I'm fine, Austin. It was just a twinge."

I grip the steering wheel even tighter. The trip to Jasper Hospital takes thirty minutes normally, but I make it in twenty. The ride here, Ally is quiet, and about halfway through the trip, she's fallen asleep.

I park in the lot and then go around to wake her up. When I pull the door open, she doesn't even budge. I undo her seatbelt and lean in, unable to resist. I press my lips to hers. "Ally, honey."

She blinks at me and then looks out at the dark parking lot. "Austin, the doctor's office is closed at this hour. If you insist I get seen, then we'll probably have to go in through the emergency room."

Just as she finishes, Brandon pulls in next to us. He comes over to the truck and looks in at Ally before holding his keys up. "Come on, I'll unlock the door."

I help Ally out of the truck, and we walk inside. The whole way, she's berating me for having her doctor come in this late at night. "Do you have any idea how much this is going to cost?" Her forehead creases as she tries to process everything. "Wait. How did you know he was one of my doctors?"

I tuck her into my side and wrap an arm around her. "Don't worry about it."

She shakes her head and starts to mumble. "Don't worry about it, he says. Sure, let's call in a doctor to come in after hours. No big deal."

I lean down and kiss her, and when I pull back, she's quiet as she stares up at me. Finally, I figured out a way to stop her from arguing with me.

We follow behind Brandon as he flips light switches in each room we pass. When we get through the lobby and the hallway, he stops at the first exam room. After flipping that light on, he opens the door. "All right, let's get you situated, and we're going to take another look."

Ally nods and gets up on the table. I stand to the side, still holding her hand as she lies back. Brandon pulls out a tray for her legs, and she's lying on her back, staring at the ceiling. "You okay?" I ask her.

She nods as she continues to stare up at the ceiling.

Brandon is doing something on the other side of the room, so I lean in to whisper to her, "Are you mad at me?"

She glares at me but finally relents. "You know I can't stay mad at you, plus, yeah, I'm worried, so I appreciate this... even if it is a little extravagant. We could have just gone to the urgent care..."

I cut her off. "Yeah, and sit there half the night. I'd rather go to someone I know and trust."

"You know Dr. Reynolds?"

Before I can answer her, Brandon comes over to us. "Okay, so tell me what's going on. You didn't say much in the text except demand that I meet you here."

Ally gasps. "Austin, you didn't!"

Ignoring her, I glare at my old college roommate. "So there was an incident tonight and—"

He cuts me off. "Is that where the blood and bruise came from?"

Ally raises up. "You're hurt? Oh my God, of course you were hurt. Are you okay, Austin? Look at me."

I ignore her. I know my ear is bleeding, but until I know Ally and the baby are okay, I'm not taking the focus off them. "I'm fine. Can you please focus here? I got into a fight. Two on one, and Ally decided to help. She swung a bat at the one. And then she had to run to get away."

I lower my head as shame fills me. "And earlier tonight, she had an orgasm."

"Austin!" Ally hollers at me. Obviously, she hadn't planned on sharing that tidbit.

I grip on to her hand and finally look at her. "He needs to know it all, baby. He's a doctor."

Brandon is holding up what looks like a wand. "Let's take a look."

Ally reaches for the waistband of her shorts, and I try to help her. "Do you need them off?"

She shakes her head. "No, just under my belly."

I pull her shorts and underwear down and then pull her shirt up. Brandon puts some jelly on her belly and then presses the wand to it. He turns a screen toward us, and I can't make heads or tails of what I'm seeing until he points everything out for me. I know he's doing it for my benefit. "Here's her head and body." He flips a switch, and the room starts to fill with a thudding sound. I look around in surprise when Brandon says, "The heartbeat is strong and steady. She's being a little active, but after the night she had, who can blame her?"

Ally is visibly relieved, and I let myself relax just a little. I bring her hand up to my mouth for a quick kiss. "Good, so everything is okay?"

Brandon cleans off the wand and hands tissues to Ally. She wipes off her belly, and finally, for the first time in the last few hours, she's smiling.

She starts to sit up, but Brandon stops her. "The baby is okay, but let me check you out."

He puts a cuff around her arm, and we wait as it starts to inflate. I'm holding my breath. I'm not sure what a good range is, so even when numbers pop up, I'm not going to know. But as soon as they appear, Brandon is shaking his head. His glare is settled on me. "I told you she had to rest. I told you that she doesn't need any stress, and what do you do? You get her involved in a street fight."

Ally comes to my defense even though I don't deserve it. "It's not his fault. He told me to stay inside and I..." She stops and looks between Brandon and me. "Wait, what do you mean you told him? How do you two know each other?"

I point at Brandon. "Remember my one year of college? This was my roommate."

"But..." She shakes her head, not understanding the connection.

Brandon puts his hand out to her, and I try not to let it affect me when he helps her sit up even though I want to punch him for doing it. "Yeah, he was a bad influence then, and it sounds like he hasn't changed any."

"He is not," Ally says angrily.

Brandon shrugs his shoulders. "Look, your blood pressure is too high. I need you to stay at the hospital tonight so we can monitor you and the baby."

Ally is shaking her head. "No, I'm not staying."

"Yes, you are," I tell her.

Her eyes snap to mine angrily. "I'm not staying here. You can't keep bossing me around." She holds her hand up when I lean toward her. "And you're not kissing me to get your way this time." She turns to Brandon. "I'll go home and rest this time. I promise."

But he's shaking his head. "I don't want to scare you, but you really need to be monitored overnight. We need to give you some meds to bring your blood pressure down, and in order to keep the baby safe, it would be better if you were here so we can monitor both of you."

Her eyes widen, and it seems that finally it's hit her. She doesn't argue again. She just nods her head in defeat. "Stay here. I'm going to go check on a room for you. You'll be up on the maternity floor, but we'll get a wheelchair to get you over there. I'll be right back." He gets to the door and turns to give me a look. "And try not to fight anyone while I'm gone."

Normally, I'd flip him off, but I'm too focused on Ally. Instead of the sassy and headstrong woman I've come to love, she looks small, overwhelmed, and unsure. "Ally, baby, you're going to be okay. You and the baby, I'm not going to let anything happen to either of you."

She grabs the front of my shirt. "Will you stay with me?"

I hold on to her and put a finger under her chin, bringing her face up to look at me. "Baby, wherever you go, I go. I'm not leaving."

She leans into me, but her head barely rests against my chest before she's lifting it up again. "Austin, oh my God, you're hurt."

She reaches for my face and turns my head side to side and gasps when she sees the cut along the side of my cheek. "Austin, oh my God, how did I miss this? How..."

"I hit my head on the rearview mirror of my car. I'm fine."

"You're not fine. You were holding your ribs earlier. You need to be checked out."

Brandon walks back into the room, pushing a wheelchair. "All right, let's go, you two. I have you in a room with two beds. We're going to get Ally situated and then we're going to get you some stitches and maybe an X-ray."

I am not going to argue with him now. I'm not worried about me, but before I argue anything, I'm going to make sure that Ally is resting and has her medication. Then I'll clean myself up. But whatever I do, I'm not leaving her side.

Chapter 11

Ally

I wake up with Austin's arm under my head. I'm pressed against his body, and his other hand is wrapped around my hip. There's a bed right next to mine, but Austin stayed in bed with me all night. I know he's not comfortable. There's no way he could be.

I pull back to look at him. Lifting my hand, I run my fingers softly through his hair and barely resist tracing my fingers across his creased brow.

Austin has been my best friend for what feels like forever. If there's anyone that I can depend on, it's him.

My life is falling apart right now, but he hasn't left my side. I've always known I can depend on him. Growing up, he picked me up when a date went wrong. He always looked out for me at parties. He made sure to include me even though I didn't really fit in with all his friends. Time and time again, he would hang out with me instead of going to the pep rallies and parties out in the fields at the edge of town. Even since we've become adults, he's been here for me. I see him all the time. I know half my clients are because he's sent them to me. He's always doing little things for me like buying me food, getting my car fixed, and things like that.

But what he's trying to do for me now is not small. What he's offering could change his whole life, and I can't let him do it. Everything is getting blurry, and it would be so easy for me to give in and let him take care of everything. The kisses we've shared, the way he made me feel last night, all if it is what dreams are made of. But just because I've been in love with my best friend for most of my life, that doesn't mean that I can just let him throw his life away because he has this need to take care of me.

His body tenses for just a second, and then he rubs his hand up and down my hip. My whole body reacts, but I try to keep it contained. "Morning, Alley Cat."

I roll my eyes at the nickname he gave me back when we were in middle school. You save a few homeless cats and nobody lets you live it down. He kisses my forehead and then untangles his arms and legs from mine before he gets up. I miss him as soon as he pulls away. He's stretching his arms over his head and yawns. "I promised the nurse I would let you sleep, and she told me I needed to be in my own bed, but I couldn't leave you last night."

I roll to my back and rub my hand up and down my belly. I'm not sure what to think about this new side of Austin. He's always been protective of me, but it seems he's taken it to a new level.

Just when I'm about to thank him, the door opens, and in walks Dr. Reynolds. "So you listened. I thought for sure you'd be throwing a party in here or something."

Austin rolls his eyes at him. "Whatever, Doc. I let her sleep."

I cut in and clear my throat. "Yeah, actually, I think it's the best I've slept in forever."

I can feel Austin's eyes bore into me, but I keep my eyes focused on the doctor. "Can we go home now?"

Dr. Reynolds picks up a clipboard and reads through it. I'm sure he's catching up on my blood pressure and other readings that the nurse documented through the night. "Okay, so we got you and the baby stable. I'm writing you a prescription to take. It will help with the blood pressure—"

I cut him off. "But the baby..."

He says, "The medicine is perfectly safe to take while pregnant. You need to take it."

I nod my head, ready to promise him anything if it means I can get out of here.

"Okay, done. I'll take it. Now can we go?"

He shakes his head and holds the clipboard to his chest. "You have to rest for two weeks. That means off your feet for two weeks. Only out of bed to shower and use the bathroom. That's it."

I'm already shaking my head in denial. I grab on to the handrail that is up on my right side and use it to pull myself into a sitting position. "I can't take off work for two weeks."

Dr. Reynolds gives Austin a dirty look and then gives me a bored one. I'm sure he never gets a good reaction when he tells a patient to stay in bed for two weeks, and I'm definitely not taking it well.

He puts his hand on top of mine. "Look Ally, I understand. You're independent. You're—"

He's cut off when Austin growls. He literally growls. The sound fills the room, and both Dr. Reynolds and I look at him. Austin is glaring at the doctor, and Dr. Reynolds lifts his hand from mine.

Finally, when he's not touching me anymore, Austin nods his head. "Go ahead, continue."

When I turn back to Dr. Reynolds, he has his arms crossed over his chest, and he's smirking. "Okay, listen. I don't want to scare you, Ally, but you need to keep the baby in there for as long as you can. I'm already sure that you're not going to carry it to term."

Alarmed, I rear back. "I won't?"

He nods. "Yeah, with your blood pressure and health, I'm thinking we may have to deliver early. But we need to try and keep her in there for as long as possible." He huffs out a breath. "Meaning you have to stay off your feet. At least for two weeks. Then we'll recheck you."

I'm shocked, and I lean back on the bed. My mind is going a hundred miles a minute as I try to figure out all the things I need to do. I need to reschedule all my appointments for the next two weeks. Damn, I need to figure out what I'm going to do about money. I have savings, but I didn't really want to dip into that with the baby coming and all. And there's at least a hundred other things I need to consider, but Austin brings me back into the present.

"After the two weeks, I can go back to work?"

He's shaking his head before I even get the whole sentence out. "We'll reevaluate you, but honestly, you're in a very active profession. You're on your feet all day. You may have to take some time off until after the baby comes."

I sputter, "But... I can't... there's no way."

Austin leans over the bed and pulls my chin up so I have to look at him. "Ally, it's going to be okay. Do you want this baby?"

I huff out a breath as a lone tear rolls down my face. "You know I do."

He nods. "I know, and you both are going to be okay." He stands up to his full height and looks at the doctor. "Okay, off her feet for two weeks... maybe more. She can do that."

I glare at him, but I know Austin, and he has the look on his face. Nothing I can say will convince him to give in. He continues, "Anything else we need to know?"

Dr. Reynolds looks at Austin. "Nope, she needs to eat healthy. The nurse will give you an info sheet with all her nutritional needs. No stress. That means no street fighting, no arguing, none of that." He walks over to me and sets the clipboard on the table next to the bed. He pinches the IV in my arm and then turns it off before putting on some gloves. "I'm going to remove this. That might help you get out a little sooner."

Austin steps forward with his hand up. "Are you sure you don't want a nurse to do that?"

I admonish him. "Austin!" as Dr. Reynolds just laughs. "I can remove an IV. I am a doctor, after all. I've had the training."

Austin squeezes my hand and wraps his other hand around our interlaced fingers. Dr. Reynolds removes the IV and puts a cotton ball and tape over the hole in my arm. Austin watches him the whole time as if he's going to screw it up. When the doctor is done, he gives Austin a look that says, *See, I told you so.*

Austin's not impressed. "Right. So she needs to rest for two weeks. We come back to see you then for more tests. We got it. I do have a question, though."

He nods. "Sure. What's your question?"

"What about orgasms? Are those bad for her or the baby?"

I gasp, and even though Austin isn't looking at me, his hand tightens on mine. Dr. Reynolds nods. "Yes, orgasms are fine. As long as she's comfortable. I would like for you to avoid penetrative sex until her next evaluation."

The doctor starts to ramble about dos and don'ts and then finally says. "Okay, the nurse will be in with your prescription and your discharge papers."

As soon as he walks out the door, I turn to Austin. "I can't take two weeks off. Heck, I can barely afford to take a day off. And what was all that about orgasms? We're not doing... that!"

He leans down until we're at eye level. He's leveling me with a heated gaze that holds all kinds of promises. But it's his words that have my nipples pebbling and my body trembling. He wraps his hand around the back of my neck, tangling his fingers in my hair. "Do you remember last night?"

I know exactly what he's talking about, but there's no way I'm going to let him know. I shrug my shoulders. "What about it?"

His eyes darken. "I feasted on you, Ally. You came on my tongue while you said my name. I've dreamt of that for a long time, but my imagination didn't even come close to the real thing."

I let out a breath. "Austin..."

I'm about to tell him that it's crazy, this whole thing is crazy. We were caught up in the moment, and things got out of hand, but he doesn't let me. He presses his lips to mine and kisses me until I can barely catch my breath before he pulls back and continues, "Did you like it, Ally? Did you like my mouth on you?"

I lick my lips, ready to deny it, but when he sees

my tongue, he groans. His voice is harder and more demanding. "Did you like it, Ally? Did you like having my mouth on you?"

I try to look away, knowing I can't lie while looking into his eyes. "My hormones are going crazy..."

He laughs. "Bullshit. I mean, yeah, I believe it about the hormones, but you liked it. You liked me touching you."

I bring my hand up to the front of his shirt. "Austin, what are we doing? What's happening?"

Chapter 12

Austin

I run my hand through her hair, fighting the urge to lean in and kiss her again. She's scared, that much is obvious, and I don't want to add to it. I wish she would let me take care of her, but with her independence, I know she won't just give up all control. Not yet.

I want to tell her I love her. I want to tell her that we're meant to be together, but she's not going to believe me. I blow out a breath and lift my hip to sit on the edge of the bed. "I wish you would see reason. This is the best thing to do—"

"Austin, I'm pregnant. Six months pregnant."

"Almost seven," I tell her with a shrug. "What's your point?"

She crosses her arms over chest. "You're

Whiskey Run's most eligible bachelor. I'm going to be some sort of buzz kill for all the women that are hoping to ride the Blaze train."

My eyes bug out of my head. "Blaze train? Really? I don't think I've heard that one before."

She shrugs. "Trust me, it's a thing. More so when all you and your brothers were single, but now that you're the last one, all eyes are on you. And you moving in a pregnant woman is not going to do anything for your bachelor status."

I just stare at her. She's going to have a thousand excuses, but none of them matter to me.

"You don't get it. If I move in with you, the women in town are going to think..."

Her voice drops off, and I tilt my head. "They're going to think what? That we're together? They should. I've told anyone and everyone that would listen that we are together. Heck, Ally. You're talking crazy. Most of the town thinks that baby is mine anyway. They think we're together."

She shakes her head. "But we're not... together, I mean."

I ram my hand through my hair and huff out a breath. "We will be."

She grabs onto my shirt and pulls me back down. "Austin, listen. I'll stay until it's safe for me to go home and be on my own. But as soon as I get the all-clear from the doctor, I'm going back home."

I'm shaking my head. "Ally, you're moving in, you're quitting your job, and you're marrying me."

Her voice gets loud in the small room. "I'm not quitting my job, and you and I are not getting married. Austin, stop talking all this nonsense. You don't marry your best friend because she got knocked up and some asshole left her to deal with it all. All you need to do is be here for me, that's all. Just be my friend. You don't have to change the whole course of your life because I screwed up. I'm not marrying you just because I got pregnant."

I try not to react. I try not to let her words affect me. I know I'm being pushy, but I had hoped there would be a part of her that wants to be married to me. I didn't think she would completely be opposed to the idea. I want to tell her that I'm not offering to marry her just because of the baby, but I know she's not going to listen or even want to hear it.

I put my hand on her shoulder. "Don't say that. Don't think that. You didn't screw up..." I stop because I recognize that look on her face. Ally is one of the most stubborn women I know, and right now, she's not listening to anything. In her eyes, she messed up. She may not realize it now, but to me, her getting pregnant was the best thing to happen. It forced me into action.

I lean toward her. "This is what we're doing."

I see the look she gives me, and I know she's not going to appreciate me just telling her what to do, so I change tactics. "If you'll agree to it, this is what I'd like to happen..."

Her face softens, and I rush on before she closes off again. "You come and stay with me for the next two weeks. Let me take care of you. You won't have to lift a finger."

She looks so worried as if she's got the burden of the world on her shoulders. "For two weeks?"

Of course I want to convince her that she's going to be with me forever, but she's exhausted. She's worried and scared, and right now is not the best time to try and convince her that she's never leaving me. "Two weeks and you rest." When she doesn't agree fast enough, I try to convince her. "Ally, you're my best friend. I can't just stand by and let you do all this on your own. I want to be there for you and for the baby. Please let me do this."

She searches my face, and she must see the sincerity reflecting in my eyes. "Okay, but if you want me out, you tell me. I can go home at any time."

I shake my head. "I won't want you out."

She shrugs. "You might. And I don't want to interfere in your life more than I already have. You don't have to take care of me or wait on me or anything. And I know I could just stay home, but I'm scared, and I'd appreciate it if I could stay with you for just two weeks. Then I'll be better, and I'll be okay on my own."

I'm not going to argue with her. She doesn't need to know that I've already arranged for someone to come in and cook all her favorite meals or that I've arranged to work from home, or that someone has been working on a guest room at my house for the last few months. I stand up and grab the bag that I brought in from Huddy's truck last night. "Okay, so I have an outfit for you to put on. Can I help you get dressed?"

She rubs her hand across her belly. "I think I can handle it."

I grab the clothes out of the bag and set them on the end of the bed. "Come on, I want to help."

She doesn't fight me. She takes my hand, and I help her to the side of the bed. I put my arms around her and untie the ribbon from around her neck. She puts her hand to the material over her chest to hold the gown in place. She's practically panting when she asks, "What are you doing?"

"I'm helping you get dressed."

She shakes her head. "I told you I can do it."

I pull the gown down her arms, and she adds her other hand to the front of her gown to hold it up.

I wrap my hand around her shoulder. "I know you can do it, but I want to help you."

She doesn't let the gown go, and I smile at her. "I've seen you naked before."

She rolls her eyes and reaches one hand out to push me in the chest. "No, you've seen me in a bathing suit. You've never seen me naked."

I grab on to her hand and hold it against my chest. I lean in until our faces are inches apart. "I'm sorry. Do you not remember last night because I sure as hell do. It's been on replay in my mind ever since."

She lifts her eyes to mine. "Yeah, I remember. But I mean, you haven't seen all this. I have stretch marks, my breasts are..."

When she trails off, I can't let her stop there. "Your breasts are what?"

"Bigger," she stutters.

"Ha ha, if you're trying to make me not want to see them, you're going the wrong way about it."

She laughs and shakes her head. "Austin..."

I grab on to the front of her gown. "Let me help

you. Come on, I'm taking care of you the next two weeks. I'm going to see you..."

She takes a deep breath, sits up a little taller, and pulls her shoulders back. "Fine. Let's do this."

I want to pull the gown away from her, but more than that, I want her to do it for me. I release my hold on her hand and gesture to it. She lets it fall and looks everywhere but at me.

I wish I could say I'm a better man, but I'm not. My eyes jerk to her breasts, and I suck in a breath. She's right. I've seen her in a sports bra and bathing suits. She's always had perfect breasts, and now if possible, she's even more desirable. I grab the shirt from the bed and unfold it, hating that I'm about to cover her up. I huff out a breath and am about to cover her when I realize she's still not looking at me. Her face is red, and she's obviously embarrassed and insecure with the whole situation.

"Ally." I say her name, but all she does is blink her eyes.

"Ally," I say again and ask her. "Can I touch you, Ally?"

Finally, her eyes flick to mine. "You want to touch me?"

She seems so surprised, and I can barely contain everything I'm feeling right now. "Fuck, Ally. You don't know how much I want to touch you right now."

I lift my hand, but I don't touch her. I wait for her to give me the green light, and the whole time, I'm holding my breath, waiting for her to respond. Finally, when it feels like minutes instead of seconds, she gives me the answer I'm yearning to hear. "You can touch me."

I lift my hand and press my finger to her hard nipple. She sucks in a breath as she arches her back, pressing herself against my hand. The power I feel right now is like nothing I've felt before. "Fuck, you're beautiful, Ally."

Before she can respond, I lean in and wrap my lips around her puckered nipple. Her hands go to my head, holding me to her as her moan fills the room.

I suckle her as I feel the weight of her other breast in my hand. I want more, but here and now is not the place. I pull back, and she's staring at me wide-eyed. I have to cover her while I'm still able to stop myself. I open the shirt and pull it over her head. I help her put her arms in the sleeves and then pull it down her body, over her baby bump.

I grab her pants and put her feet in the legs and pull them up to her thighs. With her sitting, this is as far as I can go. I put my hands on each side of her ass on the bed. I'm panting for no other reason than I'm barely hanging on. The need to completely consume her, to wrap my body around her and hold her until she promises to never leave me is unbearable. "After you've had some rest, you and I are going to have a talk."

She opens her mouth and closes it, then she finally nods her head. I help her stand up and then pull her pants up to her waist. As soon as we're both standing up, the door opens. "Dr. Reynolds has signed off on your discharge. I just need your signature on a few papers and then you'll be ready to go."

The woman is oblivious to the tension of the room. I stand up to my full height and give Ally room to sign her papers. Anxious, I sway side to side, ready to get her out of here. Ready to get her to my home... where she belongs.

Chapter 13

Ally

We no sooner get into the door of Austin's house then I remove my shoes and he's helping me up the stairs to the bedrooms. "I don't think I have to go straight to bed."

His hand is at my lower back, and he's following me up the stairs. He chuckles. "I wondered how long it would be before you tried to get out of this. Of course, I did think you'd at least make it to the bed first."

I huff out a breath. "I can't just go straight to lie down, Austin. I have to cancel all my appointments for the next two weeks. I have to figure out what I'm going to do to make money the next two weeks, and—"

I cut myself off when he leads me into his

bedroom instead of one of the guest bedrooms. "Wait, what are you doing? I'm not kicking you out of your room. I'll stay in one of the guest rooms."

He's pulling back the covers, and all I can do is stand here with my mouth hanging open. I've been to Austin's house countless times, and I know he has two other bedrooms. I figured I'd be sleeping in one of them. When he stands back up, he's coming for me. "Austin, seriously, I'm not taking your bed."

He stops in front of me and then bends over, putting one hand behind my back and the other behind my knees. He lifts me easily, and I have no choice but to just wrap my arms around his neck. "Austin, you're not listening to me."

He's watching me as he walks back to the bed. "I'm listening to you."

I let my hand slide down his chest and pat him there. "No. If you were listening, I'd be in one of your guest rooms. Or even your office downstairs. It has a Murphy bed. I can sleep there."

Right at that moment, there's a bang from the other room, and Austin frowns. He lays me down in the bed and stares down at me. The way he looks at me causes my whole body to tingle. I raise up on my elbows just as someone knocks on the open door.

"Sorry about that, boss. We're almost done in there. We'll be wrapping up..."

The voice drones on, and I sit up to try and see who it is. Austin moves, blocking me. "Sounds good, Patrick. I'll let you know when you can come back to paint the room."

The man awkwardly answers him and walks away. Austin is tense when he turns back to me. I can't resist rolling my eyes. "Austin, really, who was that?"

"Patrick."

"Yeah, I got that much. What is he doing here?"

"He's been working on the remodel of the guest room."

I take in what he said. So he's having his guest room remodeled. He's not just trying to get me into his bed or anything. He has a legitimate excuse. "Okay, fine, but you do realize that if you don't want people to know I'm in your bed, then I probably shouldn't be here. Patrick there is probably going to tell his girlfriend or wife or one of the guys he works with, and before you know it, everyone in town is going to think we're shacking up together."

He shrugs, and I should just let it go, but I don't. "Don't act like you don't care, Austin. You literally moved to hide me from being seen."

He sits down on the side of the bed. "You think I was trying to hide you... like I'm embarrassed to have you here or something?"

I shrug but don't agree even though that's exactly what I think.

He puts a hand on the bed on each side of my head. He's leaning over me, and there's a part of me that wants to pull him down over me so I can feel the weight of his body against my own. He leans down until our lips are inches apart. "I was hiding you because you're sexy as fuck. I've thought about having you in my bed for so long, and now that you're here, I don't want another man to have this image in his head." He presses his lips to mine, puts a hand to my neck, and then pulls back. "I don't want to share you, Ally."

I bite my lip and stare up at him helplessly. "What are we doing? Are we both going to sleep in here?"

He smiles. "First, I'm going to let you take a nap. I'm going to gather some things together like a laptop and lap desk. Bring your clothes in and put them away along with your bathroom stuff. Then when you wake up from your nap, I'm going to have lunch ready. Then you can catch up on a few things—from our bed."

My eyes jerk to his. "Our bed?"

He nods. "Our bed."

I have so many questions, but I can't make out one of them. I open my mouth, and all that comes out is a wide, loud yawn.

He doesn't take offense. He just laughs and stands up, pulling the covers up to my shoulders. "Rest. I'll be around."

I shake my head. "I know you need to work. I'm fine here. I'll stay in bed."

He nods and leans over to kiss me on my forehead. "Oh, I know you will. Holler or call me if you need me," he tells me as he points at my phone that's sitting on the nightstand.

I nod and snuggle into the warm bed. The sheets are crisp, and the cover is easy to snuggle under. Austin kisses my head again, then walks out of the room, shutting the door on his way out.

I try to clear my mind. I know I need to rest, but no matter what I do or how long I lie here, I know I'm not going to be able to go back to sleep. The egg burrito that Austin got me for breakfast this morning has filled up my tummy, so I would assume sleep would come easily, but it's not. I sit up in the bed and grab my phone off the nightstand. I go through my schedule and look at the next two weeks of appointments. I make a generic text message and start sending it out. I feel bad with every text I send because I'm not able to give them a reschedule date. I'm not sure when I'm going to be able to get back to work, and even though I don't want to lose my clients, I know it will be a dick move to reschedule for two weeks from now and then possibly have to cancel again.

When I've sent all the texts and my phone is dinging from all the answers, I try not to let it all get to me. Overall, people are understanding and wish me well. But there are some that are mad and feel like I've left them in a lurch.

Eventually, I turn my phone to silent and put it back on the nightstand. After sitting here for what seems like forever, I gingerly get out of bed and make my way to the bathroom. The toilet seat is down, and I try to pull the lid up, but it won't budge. There's some kind of contraption that has it locked. I tug and pull over and over, but it's not budging.

The fact that I can't pee makes me have to pee even more. Over and over I try, and it's after I've peed half down my leg that I'm able to break the latch and get the lid up. By this point, it doesn't matter. Dammit.

I shed my clothes and get into the shower. I plan

to take a quick one just to clean up, but when the spray of the hot water hits me in the back, it soothes muscles that I didn't even realize were tight. Prepared to wash my hair with some kind of mens shampoo/conditioner combo, I'm surprised when I reach to the shelf in the shower and lined up is the brand of shampoo, conditioner, and body soap I use. Even more questions pop into my head. Things I want to ask him, but I don't know if I'm going to have the guts to do it.

I finish my shower, and when I get out, I reach into the cabinet for a towel. It almost feels luxurious as I wrap one around my hair and then grab another one to wrap around my body. It's only when the towel doesn't fit all the way around that I look at myself in the mirror. I turn side to side, but no matter how I look at it, I look ridiculous. My belly is essentially hanging out, showing all my private parts. The tears start to roll, and no matter how I try to suck them back and wipe at them with my hand and then the towel, they keep coming.

I walk over to the door and lean my head against it. Well, I have two options. I can either get another towel and try to cover myself that way, or I can make a run for it and grab some clothes from Austin's drawer in the bedroom. I look down at the clothes I took off, but I know I don't want to put them back on.

I suck in a breath and know what I need to do.

I open the door and step out into the bedroom. The door is still shut, so I tiptoe across the room. I'm almost to the dresser when the bedroom door opens, and I jump with a squeal. Austin stops in his tracks as he looks from my hair that's wrapped in the towel down my body all the way to my toes. I'm practically panting when he raises his eyes back to my exposed belly.

His arms are full of clothes, and he turns, dropping them on the chair before turning back to me. "You've been crying."

I pull the towel up to wipe at my face and then struggle to cover myself again. "I'm fine."

He comes to me, pressing his body to mine. "You're not fine. You're crying. What's wrong? What happened? You're supposed to be sleeping."

I shake my head and bury my face into his chest. "I couldn't sleep. And... and you have some kind of lock on your toilet. I peed down my leg before I could get it completely off and then I showered and this stupid towel won't even go around me. I'm huge." I sob, sucking in a deep breath. "I'm about to be a mother, and I can't even take care of myself."

Before I can say anything else, he lifts me in his arms and walks over to set me on the bed. "Hold on. I'll be right back."

I watch him walk into the bathroom and almost back out. He has a brush in his hand, and he positions himself so that he's sitting behind me. He unwraps the towel around my hair and throws it to the ground. The towel around my body is useless now. It barely covered anything when I was standing up, and sitting down, it does nothing to hide all I have going on.

Austin pulls me back against him and starts to brush my hair.

"Austin, what are you doing?"

His breath grazes my ear. "I'm brushing your hair. Did you get any sleep?"

I sigh. "No, I couldn't sleep. I did cancel my appointments coming up, though."

We're both quiet as he continues to untangle my hair. I should attempt to cover myself, but I don't even care right now. I couldn't sleep earlier, but suddenly I feel exhausted. I let my body sway back until I'm settled against his chest. He leans back in the bed, pulling me with him. From this angle, my belly points out even more. I reach for the cover and pull it up over us.

He stops brushing my hair for just a second and then he starts again. "You're going to be a great mom. You know that, right?"

I shrug. I have high hopes that I'm able to figure this all out, but I definitely have my doubts. "And the thing on the toilet was something I did to childproof it. I baby-proofed the whole house."

I gasp. "You did?"

I feel his head nod. "Yeah, I did."

"Austin, you know it will be months before the baby is here, right? And then a year or two after that before she can even get into cabinets or toilets or trash cans."

He sets the brush down and then wraps his arms around me, resting both his hands on my belly. "I know that, but I wanted to be ready."

I close my eyes as I burrow deeper into him. Every part of me wants to just go along with all this, but I know that as soon as it turns bad, I run the risk of losing my best friend. And I know I won't make it the next few months, hell, the next few years without him by my side. No, I need to guard my heart. I have to.

He turns to kiss my forehead. "Also, you're not huge. I think you are absolutely beautiful and perfect the way you are."

I open my mouth to refute him but close it quickly. He shifts behind me, and I jerk to a halt when I feel it. Really slow, I say his name. "Austin."

His voice is deeper. "Yeah, baby?"

I don't try to beat around the bush. "You're hard... again."

He no longer tries to hold back. He shifts us both until we're lying next to each other. He wraps his arms and legs around me, tucking me next to him. "You need to get some rest."

I nod as I feel his hardness pressed against my belly. "What about you? You going to be able to sleep like this?"

I feel him nod. "Yeah, I'm getting used to it. If you're around, I'm hard. I'm learning to live with it."

I bury my face into his chest. *Just keep quiet, Ally. Don't say it.* But as soon as the thought comes, I open my mouth. "I could, uh, help you with that."

He groans. "Fuck, Ally. You have no idea how much I want that."

I start to reach for him, but he catches my hand with his own. He presses my open palm to his chest. "But no matter how much I want it, you're my first priority, and I know you need to rest. Let's try this. Let's see if you can sleep while I'm holding you."

I yawn, and my words slur a little as I can feel

myself falling toward slumber. "We know I can. I told you I haven't ever slept as well as I did last night."

"I thought you were joking."

I shrug and burrow deeper into him. My leg raises up his thigh until I can feel his hardness against it. "Nope. I wasn't joking." I brush my hand softly against his chest. "Thank you, Austin... for everything."

His voice is gruff, as if he doesn't like for me to give him gratitude. "You don't have to tell me thank you. I'd do anything for you."

I clench on to his shirt but don't say a word. What can I say? *Yeah, Austin, I know you'd do anything for me. Even marry me when you don't love me.* I close my eyes and force all the thoughts out of my head. I feel a little guilty, allowing Austin to do everything he's doing for me. But it's only for two weeks. Then I'll be out of his hair, and he can get on with his bachelor life... no matter how much it hurts me to do it.

Chapter 14

Austin

For almost two weeks, I've spent my days with Ally. We've watched television, talked, laughed, and hung out. I've done my best to keep her in this bed, and it's been absolute torture for me. Night after night, I've held her in my arms, tight against my body. I go to sleep with a hard-on and wake up with one too.

So many times I've wanted to taste her again, but I haven't. She's obviously troubled with everything, and I don't want to add even more pressure to her. Thank fuck, she hasn't cried again since the day she moved in here.

"You have to go into work today, don't you?"

I didn't realize she was awake. I've lain here with my arms around her, cherishing this time when she's asleep and her body melts into mine. There's no hesitancy, insecurity, or anything else when she's like this. It's just the two of us. I clear my throat. "Yeah, just for a little while. But don't worry, Elle is going to come over and hang out with you for a while."

I know she's rolling her eyes at me, and I'm not even looking at her. "I don't need a babysitter."

I rub my hand down her back. "Do this for me, Ally. I just need to go in for a little while, and I don't want to worry about you while I'm there."

She's going to argue. I'm sure of it, so I'm surprised when she says, "Okay."

I pull back so I can look at her face. "Okay? You expect me to believe you're just giving in like that?"

Her hand slides across my belly. "After everything you've done for me the past week and a half, I figure I owe you."

I kiss her hair. "You don't owe me anything, but I do appreciate you listening to what Dr. Reynolds said. Your blood pressure has been great, no headaches. Plus, I mean, I'm a lucky man." I let my voice trail off. There's a hundred reasons that I can list why I'm a lucky man, and they all have to do with having Ally in my life, in my arms, and in my bed.

"I feel like a frump."

I use my body to gently push her to her back.

Hovering over her, I search her face. "A frump? You're not a frump."

She laughs, but it doesn't hide the truth of her feelings. She honestly believes it. "I just lie here... and do nothing. I've probably gained at least ten pounds in the last week. You're going to have to probably..."

"Bullshit. You're perfect."

I expect her to laugh or smack my chest in the playful way she does, but instead her face is completely serious when she says, "You think so?" She starts to stutter. "I mean, I know I'm not perfect, but do you think... damn, I don't even know what I'm asking."

"Ask me," I demand.

She takes in a sharp breath and releases it slowly. "I just mean, do you think I'm... okay?"

I nod my head, still not sure I understand what she means. "I told you that you and the baby are going to be okay."

She shakes her head. "Forget it."

I lean into her, until her belly stops me from getting any closer. "No, I'm not going to forget it. What are you asking me?"

She blinks up at me, and her eyes that are normally a piercing green are more of a darker jade right now. They always get darker when she looks at me like she is. "Talk to me, Ally."

She blurts it out like she can't get it out fast enough. "It's nothing. I just feel fat and undesirable. It's a me problem, and I'll get over it. I have more important things to worry about than what I look like."

I thought for sure she knew. How in the world has she missed the way my cock digs into her any time she's close? Yeah, I've tried to hide it from her, not wanting to take advantage of her, but I must have done one hell of a job hiding it from her. "You're not undesirable—"

She laughs and shakes her head. I do what I've been dying to do since I pushed her to her back. I lower my pelvis until my cock is nestled between her thighs. Her legs are apart, but when she feels me slide along her inner thighs, her legs come together, and I grunt as I push even farther into her. "Does that feel like I find you undesirable?"

She lifts her hips, and I'm in agony. "Let me show you, Ally. Let me show you how much I want you."

"Yes, please..." She hesitates for just a second. "But the baby."

I cup her face. "Darling, you know I wouldn't do anything to hurt you or the baby."

She pants. "But—"

I shake my head. "No buts."

I lean back on my haunches and put my hands in the waistband at each of her hips. She lifts up without me even telling her. I pull the silky material down her legs and then toss them to the floor. I slide my hands up her legs, along her inner thighs when she stops me. Her knees come together. "Austin, wait."

I let my head fall gently to her belly. I take a deep breath and count to ten. If she pushes me away now, I have no choice but to give her some space. I raise up so I can look in her face. "The doctor said no sex... orgasms are okay."

She smiles. "I know, but I was wondering if you would... uh... kiss me."

I can't keep the smile off my face. "I plan to."

She puts her hand on my arm. "No, I mean, kiss me... on my lips."

I crawl up the bed and lie next to her until our faces are inches apart. "You want me to kiss you?"

She rolls her eyes. "Yeah, well last week I couldn't get you to stop kissing me. Of course, you were trying to shut me up."

I search her face, trying not to stare at her pretty bow lips. "You told me to quit kissing you."

She brings her hands up and caresses my cheek. "Since when do you listen to me?"

"Okay, so from now on, I'm going to kiss you when I want." When she doesn't say no or try to dissuade me, I push even further. "Anytime I want."

When she still doesn't disagree, I lean over and press my lips to hers. The kiss starts out slow and simple, but I need more. And by the way she whimpers at my touch, I think she does too. I wrap my hand around her long, soft hair and cup her cheek with the other. I tilt my head so I can kiss her deeper. When her tongue swipes along mine, I savor her taste.

I cup her breast through her shirt. "I want this off."

I pull back until I can help her get it off. She pulls the sheet up over our bodies, but it doesn't stop me. My hands are everywhere, and I know that the further we go, the more I have her close, the more I'm not going to be able to let her go.

Chapter 15

Ally

I'm panting, and my whole body feels as if it has a thousand volts of electricity going through it. I've always liked Austin's hands. When we were younger, they made me feel safe either by holding me when I was hurt or just when he would put them on me to lead me somewhere. But this is different. I still feel safe from his touch, but now I feel cherished, adored, and dare I say loved.

When he circles his lips around my erect nipple, my back arches into his touch. He's bringing out all these feelings, and they're overwhelming to say the least. I groan his name. "Austin, please."

His lips pop off my breast with a smack, but I don't have a chance to miss him because he slides down my body, kissing along the way. My heart flipflops in my chest when he kisses my baby bump, but I don't get to swoon long because before I know it, he has my legs apart, and he's settling himself between my thighs.

The anticipation is killing me. His hot breath on my skin feels way too good. Better than anything I've ever felt before. When his finger slides through my swollen, wet slit, I lift my hips to meet his touch. My body feels as if it's on fire, but he doesn't relent. Over and over, he strokes me, and with each pass over my clit, my excitement heightens.

"Austin, please, I need more."

His voice is low and meant to soothe me, but the huskiness of it has me on the edge of control. "I know what you need, Ally."

When his lips wrap around my clit and he suckles me, my whole body pulls taut. Every muscle is flexed, and I'm so close. Austin is persistent, though, because he doesn't stop. Over and over, he brings me to the edge, and when I'm so close I'm about to teeter over, he pulls back, letting the arousal edge off only to do it again. Over and over, he brings me to the brink until I'm begging him to let me come. Finally, when I can't take it anymore, he sucks my clit into his mouth, and his tongue works me ferociously until my body starts to writhe. The orgasm shoots through me and rolls through my whole body, all the way from my toes to the top of my head.

It feels like it lasts forever, but eventually, the feeling starts to abate, and I'm panting as Austin climbs up my body. His forehead is creased, and he's running his hand along my belly. "You feel okay? How's the baby?"

I blink up at him, almost incoherently. "Uh, yeah, I'm fine... she's fine."

But he doesn't seem to believe me. "No pains, no twinges... maybe I should check your blood pressure."

He's about to push off the bed when I grab his hand. "Trust me, you don't want to check my blood pressure right now."

He frowns. "Ally, honey, we need..."

I shake my head and pull him down to me. "I need to cuddle." I reach for him, and for the first time, I put my hand between his legs and cup him through his underwear. I wrap my hand around his girth, sort of taken back by the impressive length. "And I think you might need..."

His hips push into my hand, he groans, and then he wraps his hand around my wrist. "Fuck, Ally, you touch me and I'm going to come."

I can't help but laugh. His voice is strained, and his body is coiled tightly. "I think that's the whole point."

He leans his head against my chest and takes a few deep breaths. I can sense the internal struggle with him, and I'm not sure what to say to let him know it's okay. That I want to do this for him. I feather my hand through his hair. "Austin, let me... I want to."

He shakes his head. "No, honey."

I rear back, surprised. None of this makes sense. "If you don't want me to touch you, you just have to say so."

I try to push him off me, but he doesn't budge. He lifts his face to mine and kisses me. I try to hold back, but his lips hold me captive, and it's not long until I get lost in the feeling of him against me. His body is pressed to mine, but he's holding his weight off me. I feel him everywhere, and my clit is practically vibrating from the aftereffects of the orgasm he just gave me. When he finally pulls away, he holds my chin so I have no choice but to look at him. "That's all I want, Ally, to have your hands on me. But I'm not coming until I get to come inside you."

What? How is that even possible? "But that could be weeks... months..."

His lips lift in a soft smile. "Trust me. After all these years, a few months won't kill me. Especially since you've given me permission to kiss you anytime I want. I'll have your mouth... and your pussy to tide me over until your body is ready to take me."

Unease fills me. Not because of what he's saying. I want him that way more than anything, but I also know that this can't be real, or at least, I can't believe it's real. Not yet.

I stutter out the words because I don't want to tell him everything I'm thinking right now. "It doesn't seem very fair to you. So I get orgasms and you get... nothing?"

He chuckles, and his chest vibrates against mine. "Trust me, baby. When you come undone because of what I'm doing to you... I get a lot. What we're doing feels good, and even though I know what this is, I'm willing to wait and let you catch up. But eventually, we're going to have to talk this out, and you're going to have to think about the future with me as your husband and the father of your daughter."

My heart sinks. Mostly because what he's saying is everything I would want, but I'm too scared to let myself believe it's possible. "You're right...

eventually, we're going to talk about this, but I know you have to go into work today."

He levels me with a look. I feel bad because it's like I'm pushing him out the door, but the truth is, I am. I can't deal with this right now. He opens his mouth to say something but stops and shakes his head. "You're right. I do need to get to work."

I nod, but he doesn't move. "So if I leave for a few hours, can I trust you to stay in bed?"

"I already told you that I would. Plus, you have your little spies coming over."

He grins. "They're not spies. You like Elle, and eventually they're going to be your family."

I hold my hand up. 'Okay, okay. Yes, I'll stay in bed."

It's obvious he wants to say more, but he doesn't. "Okay, I'm going to shower."

I put my hands flat on the bed so he can go, but he doesn't move. Instead, he leans in and kisses me again. I'm discovering that any kiss with Austin is not just a kiss. Every time it's been an earth-shattering, soul-searching, body-shaking experience. My hands grip the sheets, fighting with myself to not hold him to me. Eventually he's going to realize I'm not what he wants, and when that time comes, I need to be ready for it.

Chapter 16

Austin

I pull into the parking lot of Blaze Distillery. I know my brothers are worried about me and Ally, but I bypass the offices and head straight to the distilleries. I don't plan on being here long, and I need to do what needs to be done so I'm not hanging out here all day. Normally, I work six days a week, and when I'm here, it's all day and half into the evening.

"How's it going, Mark?"

My assistant manager is walking toward me with a clipboard in his hands. He looks surprised to see me. "How's Ally?"

"She's as good as can be expected. She's not happy she has to stay in bed."

He laughs. "I can imagine. Take her some ice

cream and flowers when you go home. Then put her favorite TV show on and lie down and watch it with her. It will make her feel better and you'll get some brownie points."

I look at him doubtfully. "Really? TV, ice cream, and flowers are going to make her feel better?"

He holds up his left hand to show the band around his fourth finger. "You don't have to believe me, but I have been happily married for over twenty years, so I do have an idea of what I'm talking about."

I slap him on the shoulder. "Okay, you convinced me. I won't go home without the ice cream and the flowers."

"Great. You can thank me later."

"Okay, so what have I missed? I'm only going to be here a few hours. Catch me up and let me know what I need to do."

"The to-do list you sent me at the first of the week is complete. We're working on next week's orders. The new chute came and was installed. I put the old one in storage."

Stunned, all I can do is stare at him. "You're done? Everything's caught up?"

He laughs. "Yep, everything's good. Trust me, we've all missed you around here, but yeah, everything's caught up. It's been a slow week, and all the equipment has stayed intact."

We're walking next to each other through the plant, and I'm looking around, watching everyone and everything as I go. Everything is running smoothly, and it feels good to know that I can take time off and everything doesn't fall apart. "Mark, you don't have to try to cover up the fact that no one has missed me around here. You're doing a good job." His chest puffs out in pride, and I know I made a good decision in promoting him last year. "I appreciate everything you've done here, and I don't expect you to keep working like you are without getting compensated for it."

Mark stops walking and holds his hands up. "Now, Austin, you pay me really well. You pay me more than most people in this position make in the big cities."

"We may own a distillery in a small town in East Tennessee, but we're sold all across the country. We're adding new distributors every week. We make more money than distilleries in big cities." The fact he feels appreciated already makes me want to give him a raise. "It's done. I'll talk to HR, and your raise will be on your next check."

For the first time ever, Mark is speechless. He

stutters for a minute until finally he gulps and reaches for my hand. "Thank you, Austin."

I give him a firm handshake. "No thanks are necessary. Trust me when I say you're already earning it, but I do need to let you know that for the next few months, I'm cutting back my hours. I'm going to need to know I can depend on you."

Mark's jaw tightens. "You don't know this about me, but when Mary and my first son was born, Mary had complications. I spent months worried about her and Mark Jr. I swear I aged ten years in those nine months. To say I understand what you're going through is an understatement." He blows out a breath and shakes his head. "All that to say I'm here. I'll be here, and you won't have to worry about this. I got it, and I won't let you down."

The relief is instant. It's like a weight has been lifted off my shoulders. "Thank you, Mark."

I barely get the words out when I hear my brother hollering across the plant. "I knew I'd find you hiding over here."

Before turning to Ford, I assure Mark, "I'll be here a few hours to catch up on emails and stuff. Call me anytime."

Mark looks at my brother and then back at me. "Sure thing, boss."

Before I turn to Ford, I take a deep breath and let it out slowly. I know before I turn around that he's not going to be happy with me. "Hey, Ford, for your information, I'm not hiding. I just got here."

His frown deepens. "Can we talk in your office?"

Instead of answering him, I start walking through the plant. Mentally, I try to prepare myself for what's about to happen. We walk into my office, and when Ford shuts the door, I start before he can get a word in. "I'm not slacking off. I've been in contact with Mark every day, multiple times a day. I'm going over reports every day of our inventory, shipments, all of it. I'm not letting anything slide."

He puts his hands on his hips. "You think that's what I care about?"

I stutter. "Well, I uh, yeah, that's what you care about. You've always been on me about how I ran the plant, so I know that's what you're worried about."

"Bullshit."

My mouth drops, and all I can do is stare at him.

He points at the closed door. "If you think I care about that more than I care about you... or Ally and the baby... or your happiness, then you're wrong. You've completely disappeared on us. And I'm not talking about work or anything. I'm talking about how you've completely withdrawn from your brothers. You don't answer your phone, you don't tell us what's going on..."

I shrug my shoulders. "I just thought—"

He cuts me off again. "No, you didn't think. You just thought you'd handle it all yourself. We're your brothers. We want to be here for you."

I hold my hands up to stop him, but the truth of the matter is he's right. He's absolutely right. I have tried to handle all this myself. I cross my arms over my chest. "Look, I know what you're saying. The only thing that matters to me right now is Ally and the baby. I know you disagree with that, and that I should be here, but—"

"No, I fuckin' don't. Quit putting words in my mouth," he tells me with his voice hard.

My eyes about pop out of my head. He looks like Ford, but he sure as hell doesn't sound like him. "But..."

He shakes his head. "For the longest time, Blaze has been our whole life. We worked hard to build it to what it is, but the most important thing is our family." He holds his hand up. "And yes, that includes Ally. You've loved her forever, and she's always been a part of this family."

Still unsure, I lift my shoulders. "But I thought..."

He leans toward me. "You thought I'd be upset that you were taking time off to take care of your family. I know through the years, I've put all my focus on the distillery, but I know what's important, Austin. When one of us is going through something, the others step up. We stepped up when Lucas took off when Bella had the baby. We stepped in when Huddy needed help with Elle's stalker. You all stepped in when I spent the summer traveling with Lilian and Ollie. That's what we do. It's your turn now. Let us help you."

I blink at him. "I just thought you'd think I was slacking off."

"Fuck, Austin. You've worked tirelessly to make this work. The recipes and the running of the distillery has been all you. No one would think you're slacking off."

Emotions roll through me. My brothers and I have always been close, but the majority of our lives have been involved with running this company. The fact that I don't have to feel guilty for missing work or working from home takes a weight off me that I didn't realize I was carrying.

"Thank you."

He nods and then walks over to the couch in my office and sits down. "All right, so now that we have that out, talk to me. How are Ally and the baby? How are you? What can I do?"

I lean against the edge of my desk and go into the story of everything we've been experiencing. All the worries I have that I don't say to Ally because I don't want to add even more stress to her. I break it all down, and by the time I'm done, I'm slumped over in my chair feeling helpless. "I just don't know what to do. I know the answer. If she'd just marry me, her problems would go away. She could leave her neighborhood that's filled with ex-cons and drug addicts. She could work when she wants to instead of stress over not being able to work enough."

When I stop, Ford leans forward. "And?"

Confused, I ask him, "And what?"

"And she'd be married to a man that loves her and loves her baby like it's his own."

"That's a given."

He laughs, "Yeah, so she knows you love her?"

I roll my eyes at my big brother. "How could she not?" I give him a look, layered with annoyance. "Come on, Ford. This is Ally we're talking about. She's not stupid."

He nods, agreeing with me. "You're right about that, Ally is not stupid. But she has been your best friend for over half your lives. Of course her best friend is going to be there for her and try to help her."

I tilt my chin at him. "Are you saying that she thinks I'm doing this... that I'm asking her to marry me and spend the rest of her life with me because we're... because she's my best friend?"

An explosion of laughter escapes from his lips. "That's exactly what I'm saying. Maybe if you came clean and told her how you felt... told her why you've waited this long to tell her how you truly feel about her, then she might be able to make decisions based on truth instead of some bullshit idea you've put in her head that you're doing this for her own good."

I'm on the edge of my seat, ready to argue every point he just made when it hits me. He's right. Fuck, I know he is. The only way I'm going to get what I want—what we both want—is if I come clean with her and tell her how I feel. I glare at my older brother. "Does it make you happy to always be right?"

He whips out his phone. "Uh yeah, can you say that again because I'm going to record that shit."

I brace my forearms on my knees. "Fuck you. I'm not recording that. Anyone asks, I'm denying I even said it."

He shrugs and puts his phone in his pocket. "All right, so you got a plan?"

I nod. "Yeah, I'm going to stop and get flowers and ice cream and then go home. It's time Ally and I talk this out."

Ford jumps up from his seat and walks over to the door, jerking it open. "Damn right it is."

I can't help but laugh. My brother has definitely mellowed since he and Lilian got together. "Thanks, brother."

He smacks me on the back and follows me through the plant. "Anytime."

Chapter 17

Ally

Elle looks at me with hope and excitement on her face. "Are you ready now?"

I look across the room, but not at Elle. No, I look at the pile of bags that are stowed in the corner. "He shouldn't be buying me all that."

Elle goes over to pick up the bags. She carries them toward me to lay on the end of the bed. Back and forth she goes between the corner of the room and back to the bed, carrying bag after bag. Elle got here shortly after Austin left. She and Huddy carried all these bags into the room, but I told her I didn't want to open them yet. Mostly because I felt guilty accepting so many gifts from him. It's too much. Way too much.

Elle and I have eaten lunch, talked, and watched

a new romantic comedy that we've both been waiting to see, and now here we are. Elle holds the last bag up and drops it on the bed. "All right, let's talk about the elephant in the room."

I force a laugh. "You mean the mountain of bags you've laid on my bed?"

She shrugs her shoulders. "No, I mean why you don't want to accept these gifts from Austin."

I'm not ready to get into all that. "Okay, you talked me into it. Let's check it out." And then I shake my head. "I mean, I know you've already seen it all, so I can go through it later if you want."

She brings a bag closer to me. "Oh no, I haven't seen any of it. All I know is that Austin asked Huddy to meet him downtown this morning before we came over here. He and Huddy carried all this to our truck. Austin picked it all out."

My eyes about pop out of my head, and my mouth drops. "No way."

She giggles. "Yes way. Why else do you think I've pestered you all day? I want to see what he got too."

I can't help but laugh. I haven't known Elle long. She's sort of new to Whiskey Run, but as soon as Huddy met her, he pretty much claimed her. Since then, she's been a part of all the Blaze festivities, and since I'm Austin's best friend, I've gotten pretty close to her. "Okay, well see, you should have started with that. Let's open them."

She sits on the bottom of the bed and watches me. Bag after bag of clothes. All of them are cute maternity clothes. The next bag contains bras and panties. Some are practical, and some of them have my blood racing when I imagine wearing them in bed next to Austin. With a blush on my face, I quickly stuff those back in the bag but not before Elle gives me a look that says she knows exactly what I'm thinking.

When I think I've gone through them all, Elle lifts the last bag. "One more."

I take the bag from her hands and open it, looking inside before I pull it out, thinking it might be more underwear. I gasp when I look inside, and Elle asks, "What is it?"

I open the bag and pull the stuffed animal out, gasping as I take it all in. It's a huge, pink teddy bear. Probably the biggest one I've ever seen. Elle clasps her hands together under her chin. "Awwwww."

I just stare at the bear in awe. It's perfect.

"Knock, knock," Huddy hollers from down the hall. He dropped Elle and the bags off this morning, and he's back now. As soon as he walks into the bedroom, his eyes go to Elle. They both smile at each other, and it's a sight to see the love shining between them. "You ready to go?"

She bounds off the end of the bed and goes to him. She kisses him lightly and then pulls away when he tries to hold her to him. "Soon. I'm going to put all these clothes away. Have a seat, big guy."

He goes across the room and sits in the chair where all the bags were sitting moments ago. Elle starts gathering items from the bed. She grabs the bag of underwear and whispers, "I'm just going to set these on the shelf in the closet. You can try them on later." She winks, and I blush again.

When Elle goes into the closet, I look at Huddy. He's staring at me, and I shift in the bed. "How've you been, Huddy? I know Austin's glad to have you home. All the brothers are."

He grunts, and I wouldn't be surprised if that's all he said to me, but he surprises me when he tacks on, "I'm glad to be home. I wouldn't have met Elle if I hadn't come."

A smile forms on my lips. Forever, even when we were younger, Huddy was the distant, grumpy one. The fact that he's not only showing emotion but talking about it too makes me happy.

But Huddy's not really smiling. If anything, his frown at me deepens.

Unaware, Elle walks into the bedroom, grabs some clothes, and disappears back into the closet. I could just leave it alone, but the longer I sit here with Huddy glaring at me, I know that I need to say something.

"I know it doesn't look like it, but after the doctor gives me the okay, I'm moving back home."

Huddy scoots to the end of the chair. "I hope not."

I rear back. "You hope I don't move back home?"

He stands up, crossing his arms over his chest. "No, I don't."

I tilt my head to the side, trying to read his closed-off expression. "I just don't want you to think I plan on taking advantage of Austin or anything, that's all."

He takes a step toward the bed. He's still not smiling, but his face softens as he smirks at me. "You love him."

I put my hand to my round belly. "The baby is not his."

I don't know why I put it so bluntly. It's really no one's business, but for some reason I feel a need to tell him.

He doesn't look surprised by my little outbursts. "I'm pretty sure that Austin would disagree with you."

I roll my eyes. "Well, he's crazy."

"He loves you." He says it matter-of-factly. "He's loved you since we were kids."

No matter how much I want it to be true, I deny it. "He cares about me. I know he does."

Elle comes back into the room and glances between Huddy and me. She pats Huddy on the stomach, and instantly he softens into her touch. "Play nice, Huddy."

He leans over and kisses her on the forehead. "I am, baby."

She nods and grabs some more clothes before heading back into the closet. As soon as she disappears, he turns back to me. "He loves you, Ally. If you think about it, you know he does. What you need to be asking yourself is why he's never pursued you before now."

This I can answer. I've spent most of my life wondering why Austin and I couldn't be together, and I have all the answers on the tip of my tongue. "Because I'm poor and from the wrong side of the tracks—"

Huddy interrupts me. "Bullshit. You know he

doesn't care how much money you have. He's got enough money for both of you."

I shift on the bed. "Because I have no family, and family is important to him."

This time he blurts out a laugh. "Right. Are you telling me that since day one, you haven't been a part of our family? I know my brothers and I have always considered you one of us... you're our family."

Emotions surge through me, and I can feel my eyes well up. These damn pregnancy hormones are striking again. But before I can ask him why then, I hear the front door slam.

Mere seconds go by before Austin is walking into the bedroom with his arms full of flowers. His eyes find mine, and he smiles, heading straight for me. He leans over to kiss me and whispers in my ear "Missed you" before turning back to his brother. "What are you doing in here?"

Elle chooses that moment to come out of the closet. "Hey, Austin. I'm ready to go, Huddy." She walks over and leans over to hug me. When she pulls back, she explains, "I hung all the clothes. I'll see you soon, but you call me if you want me to come hang out again. I had fun today."

I lean up and hug her again. "I did too. Thank

you, Elle." She walks over to Huddy and they turn to leave. "Bye, Huddy. Thanks," I tell him.

He nods. "Think about what I said."

I nod, and when they leave, Austin turns to me. "What did my grumpy ass brother say to you?"

"Nothing. It's fine. Let's talk about you."

He sits down on the bed and leans over. "Okay, but first I need to say hi to my daughter. She's probably feeling neglected."

Before I can react, he's touching his lips to my belly and then smooths his hand across my round tummy. "I missed you too, sweetie."

I run my hand through his hair. "Austin."

He turns his soulful eyes to me. "Yeah, baby?"

I stutter over the nickname he calls me. "Uh, well, I should probably be mad. You bought me way too much stuff, especially since I can't really wear it anywhere, but thank you. It means a lot that you thought of me."

He presses his cheek into my open hand. "I'm always thinking of you."

"Thank you for the teddy bear too."

He smiles and looks over to the bear that's on the dresser. "She'll love it, right?"

I nod with a sniffle. "Yeah, she'll love it."

"So I have a surprise for you."

I'm laughing and shaking my head at the same time. "Austin, you've done so much already."

He picks up the flowers on the nightstand. "Nope, this was Mark's idea, and I think it was a good one. I told him you weren't too happy to be in bed, so he suggested I bring home flowers and ice cream and that I lie in bed with you and watch your favorite show. Here's the flowers. I have some mint chocolate chip ice cream in the freezer. I talked to Brandon, and he said a small serving would be fine, and we can watch whatever you want to watch."

I tilt my head. "You called the doctor to see if I could eat ice cream?"

He acts as if it's not a big deal. "Yeah, it wasn't on the nutrition list, so I had to be sure."

"And I get to pick..."

He nods. "You get to pick. It doesn't matter to me as long as I get to lie next to you. I'll even watch one of those romance movies you like so much."

I hold my breath. I'm used to nights out at the Whiskey Whistler or going out with my friends. But what he just suggested sounds like the absolute perfect night to me. "I think Mark sounds like he's pretty smart."

Austin laughs. "He would agree with you. I

figure I should listen to him since he's been married over twenty years."

My heart is thundering in my chest. Not just because of the ice cream and the flowers and everything else he's done for me but because of how he makes me feel. With him, I feel loved and cared for, and it scares the hell out of me.

I want to ask him if what his brother told me is true. I'm beginning to think it's possible. In this moment. I promise myself I'm going to see where this goes. I'm not going to make any promises or even give in to his pressure of marriage, but I am going to enjoy this... for however long it lasts.

Chapter 18

Austin

I jerk awake with a groan. I was having the most illicit dream, and now that I'm wide awake, I realize it wasn't a dream. I open my eyes just as Ally wraps her lips around my hard cock.

My hips jerk, and I plunge deeper into her mouth. "Fuck, Ally."

She smiles around her mouthful, and her hand wraps around the base of my girth. She takes me deeper, and that's when I come to my senses. She's pregnant and supposed to be resting. She's not supposed to be on her knees, servicing me.

I grab her by the shoulders and pull her up the length of my body. I lay her on her side and curl my body around her. "Ally, baby, you're supposed to be resting."

She arches her back, pressing her lower body into me. Her T-shirt has ridden up, and her panties do nothing to block me. She keeps moving until my manhood is positioned between her thighs. My groan fills the room, and I back off the bed, falling to my knees on the floor. The only way I'm going to be able to stop myself is to put some distance between us. "We can't. You know what the doctor said, and I'm not taking any chances in hurting you."

She leans up on her elbow, and I try to look away from her body, but it's nearly impossible. Even now with her mussed hair and oversized T-shirt, she's the most beautiful woman I've ever looked at.

She sits up, grabs the hem of her shirt, and pulls it over her head. She starts to ramble. "You bought me everything I could possibly need yesterday, but you know what you didn't get me?"

My mouth is dry, looking at her rounded breasts begging to be touched. "What?" I croak.

"Pajamas. Those were noticeably missing, and you know what I think?"

My hands go to her panty-covered hips, and I drag in a breath. "What? What do you think?"

She leans toward me. "I'm thinking you don't want me to sleep in pajamas. I mean, you sleep in your underwear. Maybe I should sleep in mine."

"Fuck." I raise up on my knees and bring my hands to her cheeks. "I'm all for you sleeping naked next to me... after the doctor gives you the okay to have sex. I won't be able to resist otherwise."

"Austin," she whines. I look at her with surprise, and she throws her hands up.

"What? You think I sound like a child? I know I do, but I need this... I need you."

I move to sit up on the bed. It's painful to move with my cock as hard as it is, but I'm not worried about myself in this moment. I'm worried about Ally.

"Our appointment is today. Let's see what the doctor says because no matter how much I want to be inside you, I won't do it and risk you and the baby."

She releases a strangled breath. "Okay."

I lift her chin up. "Don't get all up in your head. I'm not saying no because I don't want you or want this to happen between us. I'm saying no until we know it's okay and safe for you."

Her hand goes to my bare chest. "Okay. But what about you? I can take care of you—"

My forehead creases, and my hands clench into fists. "Nope. Get up, let's go."

I stand up and walk across the room. When I turn to look at her, she's sitting up staring at the clock on the nightstand. "Austin, it's eight in the morning. Our appointment is not until eleven-thirty."

I put my hand on the door to stop myself from going back to her. In all these years, she's never reached for me, and mere minutes ago, she was initiating sex. It took everything in me to stop, and even now, I'm on the very edge of control. "I'm going to fix you breakfast, and I'm calling the doctor to move up the appointment."

"Austin, you can't do that."

I laugh because she should know by now I can do whatever I want. "It's happening. Get ready, baby. I'm going to bring breakfast up and then we'll go."

I walk out of the room before I change my mind.

I make a quick meal of eggs, whole wheat toast, and oatmeal with apples and raisins in it. By the time she eats and we both get ready, we make it to the doctor's office at ten.

We barely get seated in the waiting room and a nurse is calling our name.

The nurse weighs her, takes her vitals, and sends her to the bathroom with a cup.

I'm sitting in the room when she comes to join me. "Everything okay?"

She nods. "Yep, they said Dr. Parks will be in soon."

She no sooner gets the words out than an older doctor walks in the room. I take in the white-haired man, measuring him on sight. If he's the one that delivers the baby, I need to know he's capable. I hold my hand out. "Hello. I'm Austin Blaze."

He lifts his head up and looks at me through the lower lens of his glasses. "Blaze, huh? Is that why I was notified that Dr. Reynolds would be joining us today?"

"Austin," Ally protests.

I squeeze her hand reassuringly. "I hope that's okay with you, Dr. Parks. Since he has an office in Whiskey Run and here in Jasper, we'll have an option that is close if we need it. Ally wants you to deliver our baby, but I just want to make sure we're covered no matter what."

The doctor measures me with a look. "I guess it will be fine. I mean, if you're willing to pay two doctors for your, uh—"

I cut him off. "Wife. Ally and I are getting married."

For the first time since he's laid eyes on me, he gives me a look of approval. "Right. Like I was saying, if you're willing to pay for two doctors to care for your wife, then who am I to stop you?"

I shake his hand. "I appreciate that, Dr. Parks. Ally speaks very highly of you."

At that moment, there is a brief knock, and Brandon pokes his head in the door. "Sorry I'm late. Well, of course, I'm not really late. I'm an hour and a half early since the appointment got moved up—with short notice, I might add."

I just shake my head and laugh. Brandon is a hell of a doctor, but he's going to be a pain in the ass, I can tell. "Well, it's a good thing I'm paying for your time. Thanks for coming."

We shake hands, and finally both doctors turn their attention to Ally. They ask all the questions. How she's feeling. What her diet has been like. If she's had any pains. And the list goes on and on.

They examine her and check the baby, and a calm comes over me when the small room fills with the thump, thump, thump of the baby's heartbeat.

After the examination, Dr. Parks hands tissues to Ally. "Why don't you get cleaned up and a nurse will come get you. We'll meet in my office to go over everything."

As soon as Dr. Parks and Dr. Reynolds leave, I take the tissues from her and wipe her belly. "You okay?"

She struggles to sit up, and I wrap my arm

around her to help. With a huff, she says, "I wish you'd quit asking me that."

"I'm sorry," I tell her instantly. I've been reading up about pregnancy and the way the book described how a mom-to-be feels has me wanting to apologize to her and do whatever I have to do to make her life easier.

She looks at me guiltily. "Don't say you're sorry. You've been great, Austin. This is all me."

I tweak her nose. "You're just sexually frustrated. So am I. I get it."

She doesn't deny it. When the nurse comes to get us, we walk down the hallway, hand in hand. When we get to the office and take our seats, it's obvious the two doctors have been reviewing the results and talking about the plan.

"How's Ally and our daughter?"

I'm blunt and to the point. Ally squeezes my hand, but I'm not interested in waiting any longer.

Dr. Parks nods. "Right. Well, Ally, your blood pressure has improved. The meds are helping. Your urine test improved greatly from two weeks ago. All in all, your numbers look good."

I can tell by the way they're looking there's more. "But?" I ask them, dreading the answer.

"Well, Dr. Reynolds and I conferred, and we

both agree that it's in the best interest of the baby and you, Ally, if you take the remainder of your pregnancy off of work. If you had a desk job or even a job where you weren't on your feet all the time, then it would be fine, but with your occupation, that's not a possibility."

I look at Ally, waiting for her to deny them and then I'll have to intervene, but she surprises me when she nods her head. "If you think that's what's best, that's what I'll do."

She's not happy about it, and I knew she wouldn't be. She's so independent, and I know it's killing her right now. Her face screws into a scowl. "Do I have to stay in bed all the time?"

They are both shaking their heads, but it's Dr. Reynolds that answers. "No, you don't. You'll have to monitor your blood pressure. If there are any spikes or any changes at all, you need to come to our office and be seen immediately. If it gets high again, you will be put on bed rest until after the baby comes."

She gulps. "Okay."

But Dr. Reynolds isn't finished. "I don't want to scare you, but this doesn't mean you can just go back to the activity level you were at before. You can get up and go out, but you have to get plenty of rest. I really want you to understand that at the point you're at in your pregnancy, rest and no stress is the most important thing."

She nods her head. "I got it. I promise. I'm going to take care of myself and the baby."

I reach over and squeeze her hand.

"Okay." Dr. Parker stands up. "Do you have any other questions or concerns?"

Ally nods and doesn't even blink when she asks him, "Yeah, I have one. Can I have sex?"

Dr. Parks nods. "Yes, sex is actually a good way to relieve stress. Nothing crazy, but yes, sex is fine."

He goes on to answer her question in detail, but it's all a blur to me. All I know is that we've been given the green light. I'm finally going to have Ally how I've always wanted her. She's going to be mine in every sense of the word.

Chapter 19

Ally

Austin and I are quiet the whole way home. At first, I wonder if I overstepped by asking the doctor if it was okay to have sex. Of course, I was thinking of Austin, and for just a brief second, I wonder if he's changed his mind. But then I remember the way he held me and the way he made me feel, and I know I'm not wrong about this. Austin wants me, and if I get my way, he's going to have me.

He pulls into the garage, and I step out of the car. Austin is waiting on me at the front of the car. I avoid his gaze because I know he'll see the blush on my cheeks.

I walk past him, kicking my shoes off at the front door.

I get two steps and Austin reaches for my hand,

pulling me to a stop. He turns me and pulls me against his chest. I land with a thud, and he encircles his arms around me. "Do you want to talk about the doctor appointment?"

I blink up at him. "What about it?"

He smiles as he brushes my hair back and tucks it behind my ear. "About how you asked if you could have sex."

My mouth falls open. "Oh yeah, that."

He leans his head against mine. "Yeah, that. You can't say something like that and then expect me to forget about it."

I don't answer him, and he weighs me with a look. "Unless you've changed your mind."

I stiffen my back and let my hands trail up Austin's stomach, across his hard abs and up to his chest. I palm his pectoral muscles feeling his nipples pebble through his shirt under my hands. "I haven't changed my mind. I want you, Austin."

He groans and runs his hands down my back to my ass, pulling me up against him. "Well, that's good to know because I've been hard ever since."

I ignore the way the swell of belly presses into his hard stomach. I curl my hands around his neck, threading my fingers through his hair. "Are you sure about this? This body is—"

He cuts me off. "Perfect. Your body is perfect."

I look at him doubtfully, and he is quick to reassure me. "Trust me, I'd know. I wake up hard next to you every morning. Why do you think that is?"

I shrug, but he doesn't let me get away with it. He leans down and looks into my eyes. "I'm hard because I wake up with your body pressed to mine. You always have your leg laid over mine, lining your pussy right up against me." I let out a slow whistle. "You don't know how many times I've thought about sliding your panties to the side and pushing inside you, making you mine."

I can't help it. With awe in my voice, I ask him, "You really want me, don't you?"

He chuckles. "Fuck, yeah, I do."

He leans over, wrapping one arm behind my back and the other behind my knees. I stop him from picking me up. "Austin, I'm too heavy... I can—"

He cuts me off as he swings me up in his arms. "Again, you're perfect. How many times do I need to tell you before you believe me?"

I lean my head against his chest. "Well, it's not like I'll get tired of hearing it."

He climbs the stairs and doesn't even get short of breath.

When we get to the bedroom, he lets me down until my feet softly land on the floor. He stands in front of me. "Can I undress you, Ally?"

I smile at him. "Those are four words I thought I'd never hear from you."

"I want to fuck you."

My eyes widen. "Or those."

I could be shy. I could tell him I'm going to undress myself and hide under the covers, but I don't want to. The way I feel when I'm with him makes me want to be uninhibited. I push him until the back of his knees hit the bed and he sits down.

I reach for the hem of my shirt and start to pull it up. I get halfway up my belly and stop. "Are you sure about this, Austin? We can turn off the lights, and you can still have your way with me."

He's staring at the bare skin of my midriff. "Oh no, I want to see it all."

Reassured, I pull the shirt over my head and let it fall to the floor.

My chest is practically vibrating as I reach behind me and undo my bra, letting the straps fall off my shoulders and then to the floor.

Austin licks his lips and demands, "More."

I undo the button of my pants and pull them down my hips. When they get below my knees and

I can't bend over any more, I kick them from my legs.

In nothing but my panties, I reach for Austin, but he's shaking his head. "No, more."

I stand in front of him. "You want them off, you take them off."

He doesn't hesitate. He puts his hands at my hips and pulls my panties down. He drops them to my feet, and I kick them away.

His gaze travels the length of my body, up and down.

His hands tighten on my waist, and he brings me forward until I'm straddling his legs with my knees on the bed.

His hands are everywhere, and when his mouth opens over my breast, my whole body comes alive.

I wrap my arms around his neck, holding him to me as I gyrate my hips back and forth. The feel of his rough jeans against my skin is good, but I know what would be better.

I pull at his shirt, and he releases my breast just so I can pull the shirt off and then he moves to my other breast.

"Austin, your pants. I need your pants off."

He groans and lifts his hips up.

I climb off him and sit to the side, reaching for

the button of his jeans. He pushes my hand away and then stands up to take off his pants and underwear in one quick swoop.

It would almost be comical how fast he was about it if I wasn't stunned by the very thick, very erect, manhood that is pointing right at me.

Chapter 20

Austin

She's staring at my cock, and I swear my shaft twitches under her gaze.

She reaches for me, wrapping her hand around my girth, and I shamelessly shove my hips forward, letting her jack me from tip to root.

Her mouth is hanging open as she stares at me. "Austin, that is—"

I cut her off. "Why do you look surprised? You literally had that in your mouth this morning."

She shakes her head, "Yeah, but it was early morning, and there were sheets involved. This is different. That is big!"

I tighten my hand around hers. "This is going to fit perfectly in your pretty pussy."

Her eyes jerk to mine, and I force a smile. "Do you trust me?"

She rolls her eyes. "You know I do."

We stroke my length again. "I know, but I felt like you needed to hear it. I'm not going to hurt you. No matter how bad I want you, I would never hurt you."

She nods and strokes me again.

I shove her hair back from her face, wanting to see her. "I'm thinking you can be in control. I'll lie back, and you can be in complete control. You decide how deep you want to take me."

She looks at my length and back at me. "Okay."

I crawl into the bed and lie on my back. She stands up next to the bed, staring at my thighs. I grab her hand, and even though it's the last thing I want to say, I give her another chance to change her mind. "Are you sure, Ally? There's no going back from this."

She sucks in a breath and nods her head. "I'm sure. I don't want to go back."

She lifts her leg to straddle me, and I swat her hip. "That's right, pretty girl. No going back for us."

She sits astride me, gently rolling her hips back and forth. I'm not inside her where I'm dying to be, but this feels good too. She's wet, and the slick folds of her pussy are cradling my cock as she moves back and forth.

With each soft thrust, the tip of my cock hits her clit, and she jerks on contact. "You like that, don't you?"

She nods and does it again.

Her breaths are coming in pants, and I know she's exerting herself more than she should. "Slow down. There's no rush. We have all night."

She leans forward, and I cup her face, pressing my lips to hers. Our kiss is electric, and I pull her to the side so she can lie in my arms while I love on her.

My hands cup her breast, pressing a thumb across her aching nipples. Then I slide my hand down her belly to her inner thighs. Her legs widen, and I trail my fingers through her slit. Her hips rock back and forth as I circle her clit.

"I need you, Austin."

"I got you," I tell her.

I lift her leg, bringing it over my thighs, nudging my hips toward her. I want her to have control, but I know being on top was exhausting for her. "How about like this? This okay?"

She reaches between us, wrapping her hand

around my cock and then shifting her body around until she can position me at her core.

It takes everything in me to stay still, but I do. It's only when I'm inside her and her pussy is wrapped around me do I let out a struggled breath. "Yes," I tell her.

She shifts again, pulling me in deeper, and I groan, letting my head fall until our foreheads are pressed together.

"Deeper, Austin. I need you deeper."

I wrap my hand around her thigh, pulling her closer to me as I angle my hips. I'm deep now, and the heat of her wrapped around me makes me want to go deeper. "You okay?"

She nods. "Yes, oh yes, I'm good. I've never been better. Please don't stop, Austin. I need it all. It feels so good."

I go deeper and watch her closely. I keep going inch by inch until I'm buried inside her. "I'm going to move, okay?"

She moans and beats me to it as she pulls her hips back and then slams them forward. With my hands at her hips, I thrust in and out of her. She's untamed as she rolls her hips in circles then front to back, but I'm steady as I wait for her to find what works for her.

When her pussy starts to squeeze me and my cock feels like it's in a vise, I press my finger to her swollen clit and strum it back and forth over and over.

Her moans get louder. Her pussy gets wetter, and her thrusts get erratic. It's almost too much.

"Yes, yes, don't stop. Yes," she begs as her climax takes her over the edge. I race with her, shooting my release inside her, claiming her as mine.

We're both breathless, but I can't let her go. I roll to my back, pulling her across my body. We're still joined, and I wish I could stay in this moment forever.

Shoving her damp hair from her face, I look into her eyes. I'm searching for any kind of regret, but I don't see any. "You okay?"

She nods with a big smile on her face. "Do we get to do that again?"

I can't help it. I wasn't expecting that at all. I laugh out loud. "Baby, we can do that any time you want."

She rests her head on my chest, and I lay my head back on the pillow. Only a few minutes go by, and I hear her mumble something. I'm almost positive she says "forever," but I convince myself that I'm hearing things.

I kiss her forehead and let myself imagine a future where I have the one thing I've always wanted. It's almost too good.

Chapter 21

Ally

My phone rings, and a smile forms on my face. Of course, I think it's Austin. He had to go into the plant this morning, but he's already called a few times. He'll have some excuse of why he's calling, but we'll both know it's just because he's wanting to make sure I'm resting.

"Hello."

"Ally."

I pull the phone from my ear and look at it. That's not Austin, and my stomach rolls knowing who's on the other end of the line. My voice is hard. "What do you want?"

"I thought we should talk."

I put one hand on the kitchen counter and lean on it. The happiness and joy I felt just moments ago is gone now. "We did talk, and you said plenty. Actually, I don't think we have anything else to talk about."

He raises his voice and says in a rush, "I want to talk about the baby. My baby. I have rights, Alison."

Every muscle in my body reacts, and my heart springs to battle. "We talked about this, and you said you don't want anything to do with the baby. You... you said you weren't even sure the baby is yours."

"So it's not mine."

I grit my teeth. "You are the biological father."

"Okay, then, I'm in town. Let's meet. Where are you at? I'll come there."

"No!" I say quickly. "I'll meet you in town at the Whistler."

We say our goodbyes, and I pace back and forth across Austin's living room. My first thought is to call Austin. He'd want to know, and I also want to talk to him about this. But he's barely gone into work at all since I've been here, and I know if I call him, he's going to come straight home.

I grab my purse and drive into town. My mind is going a hundred miles a minute. I know nothing good is going to come of this, but I have to at least try. Since the first time I told him I was pregnant and he refused any responsibility, I've thought about asking him to give up his rights to my child. That's what is pushing me to drive across town.

Because it's the middle of the day, I'm able to park right in front of the Whiskey Whistler. Taking a deep breath, I pull open the door to my car, put a protective hand over my belly, and make my way inside. I look around and find Gregory immediately, and he's downing a pint of beer.

When I get to the table, he looks at my belly, and his eyes widen. "Uh, you've put on some weight—"

I cut him off. "Yeah, being seven months pregnant will do that to you. So what do you want, Gregory?"

He tilts his head, and I shift in my seat the way he's looking at me. He points at my belly that is protruding over the top of the table. After crossing his arms on the table, he leans forward and just stares at me.

I don't look away even though the longer I sit here, the more I wish I hadn't come. When he doesn't answer my question, I continue, "Forget it, I don't need to know what you want to talk about. I have a few things I'd like to discuss with you."

His lips lift in a smirk. "Oh yeah? What's that?"

I straighten my back and hold my hands together

on the table in front of me. "I'd like for you to sign your parental rights over to me."

His eyes widen, and it's obvious I've surprised him. He holds a hand up to stop me when I start to talk again. "Wait. So you are wanting me to relinquish my rights... to my child."

I don't even hesitate. I want that more than anything. "What do you mean your child? You said yourself it wasn't yours. You said there's no way this could even happen even though we both know the condom broke. But regardless, yes. That's exactly what I want. I want you to sign over your rights."

His forehead creases. "So you came to me months ago and wanted me to be involved in"—he waves his hand toward my belly—"this, and now you decide that you don't want me involved."

I cross my arms over my chest and nod my head. "Yes." I could argue with him and tell him that I never asked him to be involved in any of this, that I just wanted to let him know that he was going to be a father, but it's pointless. All I care about now is getting what is best for my daughter. It may have taken me a few months to figure it out, but it's more than obvious that both my daughter and I will be better off without Gregory.

He leans back in the chair. "Did you know that

your friend Austin is telling everyone that you and he are getting married and that the baby is his?"

I grit my teeth. I should have known that the gossip would make it to him. He may live in the next town over, but if he spends any time in Whiskey Run, heck here at the Whiskey Whistler, all he has to do is ask about me, and anybody would be happy to tell him about Austin and our little family. "Yes, I'm aware."

He taps his finger on the tabletop, staring at me. There's a new glint in his eyes, and I move my hand back to my belly in a protective gesture. I'm not comfortable with the way he's looking at me.

"Hey there, what can I get you... uh, two?"

The same waitress from book club night stops at the table, and I can tell she's surprised to see me sitting here with anyone besides Austin. I force a smile to my face. "Thanks, Megan, but I'm good. I'm about to leave."

She nods her head and looks at Gregory. "Can I get you another beer?"

Gregory nods his head. "That would be great."

Megan gives me one last pointed look. "Let me know if you change your mind... if you need anything, just let me know."

"Thank you."

I wait until she's walked away from the table before I turn back to Gregory. "So I can get you the papers later today. All you'll need to do is sign them. Does four o'clock work for you?"

His smile widens, and for the first time, I notice that the look on his face is just blank. It's like there's no life in his eyes. "No, four o'clock does not work for me. Actually, I won't be signing any papers. I've changed my mind."

I swear my heart stops beating for a few seconds, and I suck in a breath. "What do you mean you won't be signing over your rights? You don't even want this baby."

His jaw tightens, and I can't look away from him. I'm wondering again what I ever saw in him. Up until the day I told him I was pregnant, he was a decent guy. It seems that ever since then, there was a switch that flipped.

Megan comes and sets the beer on the table, giving me a look. I force a smile to my face even though it's the last thing I want to do. She walks away, and I ask Gregory, "Well?"

He leans in and lowers his voice. "Alison, you're a hairdresser. You live in a neighborhood full of drug dealers, and you live pay check to paycheck."

A glimmer of unshed tears forms in my eyes, and

I suck in a breath, refusing to let them fall. "Are you saying that poor people shouldn't have babies?"

He smirks at me, and it takes everything in me not to smack him in the face. He lifts his shoulders in a shrug. "I'm saying that if a judge looks at me—" He points at himself, and I glance at his dress shirt, tie, and jacket before returning to his face, and he's now gesturing at me. "And then at you, I'm pretty sure he won't have any trouble making the decision that a child would be better off with me."

My mouth drops. "You don't even want the baby."

He shrugs. "I do now."

I cross my arms over my chest. "And what changed your mind? How much have you had to drink anyway?"

He's not offended. He takes a big gulp, finishing off the beer that Megan had just set down. "The baby is going to be mine, Alison. Maybe I should bring you some papers to sign."

I fix him with a lethal look. Taking a deep breath, I struggle to get out of my seat. Once I'm standing, I don't worry about how loud my voice is. "You are not getting my baby."

He just laughs, and the sound goes all through me.

I turn on my heel and walk out of the Whistler. I get in my car and drive around the block, pulling into a back alley. I wish I was home. Hell, I wish I'd stayed at home. I bang my fists on the steering wheel, and when that doesn't make me feel any better, I lay my head on it and let the tears fall. I can't lose my baby. I already love her so much, I can't imagine letting anyone have her. Heck, I can't even imagine sharing custody of her with someone and having to give up some of my time with her.

I try to stop the tears, but no matter what I try to tell myself, they don't stop. I reach for my purse, and after minutes of trying to find my phone, I grab it up and toss the contents on the passenger seat.

I open the phone and do the one thing I should have done when Gregory called me earlier. Taking a deep breath, I dial Austin's number, and when he answers, just hearing his voice causes the tears to flow harder. "Austin... I need you."

Chapter 22

Austin

"I'm on my way home."

I'm already running from the plant. Any and every bad thing that could have possibly happened goes through my head, but the only thing that matters is that I get to Ally. "Ally, honey, please calm down," I plead with her even though I'm anything but calm.

When she takes a deep breath, I continue to try and soothe her. "Ally, baby, take a breath and try to calm down. I'm coming home. You just need to—"

"I'm not at home."

I was about to pull out of the parking lot toward our home, but instead, I slam on the brakes and hold in a curse because I have no idea where she is. "Ally, baby, where are you?"

She sobs. "I'm in the alley... behind the Whistler."

I don't ask any questions even though I want to. "Okay, baby. Good, good, you're close. I'll be there in five minutes, but I need you to calm down and take a few deep breaths, okay?"

"Okay," she says with a sigh.

"Should I have Brandon meet us at the hospital?"

"No!" she says. "No, I'm fine. I'm okay... I just need you."

I run through a red light, and when I'm only two blocks away, I tell her, "Okay, baby. I'm almost there, okay?"

"Okay."

Fuck, I slam my hand onto the steering wheel, wanting to hear something from her besides okay.

I turn the corner and hit the brakes. She's parked in the middle of the alley. I slam my SUV into park and bolt out the door, sprinting to her car. As I'm approaching, I see her head is lying on the steering wheel. "I'm opening the door, baby. I'm here," I tell her, because I don't want to startle her.

I pocket my phone, and she lifts her head as I open her door. When I see her, two things happen. I feel sick and utterly relieved in the same breath. I squat down until I'm beside her and cup her face in my hands. "Ally, baby, talk to me."

She nods. "I will, but can you take me home, please? I just want to go home."

I reach into her car and put one hand at her back and one under her legs. She doesn't resist me when I lift her out. Kicking her door shut, I carry her back to my SUV. When I get her in, I lean in and pull the seatbelt across her lower belly. "Ally, let me call Dr. Reynolds. Let's make sure you and the baby are okay."

She leans her head back on the chair. "I'm fine, please, Austin. I'll tell you everything, I just want to go home."

I kiss her forehead and then shut her door. My thoughts are everywhere, but I rush around to the driver's side and get in. Neither one of us talks the whole way home. I pull into the garage and help her inside.

She sits on the couch, and I help her by sitting on the coffee table and bringing her foot up in my lap. I remove one shoe and then the other.

When I help her lie back on the couch, I cover her up and then sit back down on the coffee table, leaning over her.

When she opens her eyes and turns her head to

me, she looks so sad it guts me. My voice is a croak and filled with emotion. "Talk to me, baby."

She sucks in a breath. "Gregory called me and asked if I would meet with him."

I can't help the sense of betrayal that goes through me. "You went and met him?"

She nods and puts her arm over her eyes. I want to ask her more, but the need to make sure she's okay outweighs all the questions I have. "Do you have a headache?"

She nods her head, and I'm up in search of the blood pressure monitor. I'm running up to the bedroom, telling her what I'm doing the whole time. I'm back to her in a minute, and I wrap the cuff around her arm.

Anxiously, I wait for the reading and breathe a sigh of relief when it's on the higher side of normal, but at least it's normal. "It's normal. Do you want some Tylenol?"

She shakes her head side to side, and I get nervous when she goes quiet again.

I let her sit quietly, trying to be patient even though it's the last thing I want to be. When she doesn't say anything, I can't stop myself. "Do you love him?"

She pulls her arm from over her face. "What are you talking about?"

My chest seizes up. "I'm just asking you, Ally. He obviously upset you, and—"

She cuts me off. "He said he won't sign over his rights."

I hiss out a breath. "You want him to give up his rights?"

She looks at me as if I'm crazy. "Of course I do." She struggles to sit up, and I grab her arm to help her sit up. "What? You thought I wanted him back?"

I hunker down on my knees to get closer to her. "No, I mean I hoped not, but Ally, honey, I'm just trying to figure out what's going on, that's all. Is that why you're this upset? He won't sign the papers?"

She levels me with a glare. "No, I mean, of course I want him to, but he won't do it. The reason I'm so upset—" She sucks in a deep breath, and the way she lets it out, slow and controlled, tells me that whatever she says next, I'm going to want to kill the asshole. "Gregory said he can talk to a judge... that, uh, he wants custody—full custody—of my daughter."

"That won't fuckin' happen."

Her eyes widen, and the way she looks at me tells me that she wants to believe what I'm saying, and there's no way I'm going to disappoint her. "Listen to me, Ally. I promise you, there is no way he is going to get custody of our daughter."

"You can't promise that."

I put my hands to her belly. "Ally, listen to me. I know we've been through this over and over, but I need you to marry me. No matter what, I'm going to protect you and our daughter, but it would be so much easier if you had my last name."

She reaches for me, cupping her hand along my jaw. "Austin..." She searches my eyes, frowns, and then her jaw tightens. "Do you really think that if we're married, that would stop him from getting custody?"

I cover her hand with my own. "Ally, what I'm saying is that no matter what, he is not getting our baby. I won't let that happen whether you and I are married or not. But I want you to be my wife. I want to be that baby's real father."

She sobs and nods her head. "Okay, I'll marry you." She holds her hand up. "But anytime you want to move on, you want this to be over, I understand. I'm not expecting forever."

I'm not going to argue with her. All that matters now is the fact that she agreed to marry me. I lean my head in her lap and hug her to me. "You won't regret it, Ally. I promise you'll never regret agreeing to marry me."

I pull back and rise to my feet. "Come on. I'm going to run a bath for you, and then we're going to lie in bed and rest."

She pulls me by the collar of my shirt. "I need you, Austin. I don't want to rest. I want to forget about my day today, and I want you to help me forget about it."

I lift her into my arms. "Baby, by the time I'm done with you, you're not going to think twice about today. All you're going to think about is how I make you feel."

She leans her cheek against my chest, and I carry her up the stairs. She's finally given in. I'm going to make sure she and the baby are safe. And I'm going to get what I want. I ignore the twinge of guilt that I feel. I know I have things I need to tell her, but I'm going to do it another time.

Chapter 23

Ally

Austin offered to throw a huge wedding. He wanted to buy me a dress and have a big party, but I talked him out of it. I just wanted it done. That was a month ago. I know that officially being a Blaze is going to offer a level of protection to me and the baby, and that's why I did it, but there's a part of me that knows I have more reasons for wanting to marry Austin.

But as soon as I start to think of those reasons, I shut them down. I've told myself over and over I'm not going to get caught up in all this, but I can't help it. The way he makes me feel. The way he has made sure to take care of me and the baby... damn... how could I not fall completely, head over heels in love with him?

So now here I am, completely in love with my best friend, who is now my husband, and I need to act like I'm not. Austin has never been one for commitments. I've seen him date throughout the years, and as soon as a woman wanted more, he'd be out the door. Nope, I'm going to do my best to play it cool.

I'm staring at the ring on my finger when Austin nudges me. "You regretting it?"

I ignore the stares that we get from the other people in the waiting room. I hold my finger up. The ring is enormous. I told him over and over that he could get me something small, but this is what he gave me instead. Since that day a month ago, I've caught myself staring at it over and over, daydreaming. It sure doesn't look like a ring you give someone that you know you plan on divorcing someday. That's the thought that always enters my mind. "No, I'm not regretting marrying you. How could I? You've been the perfect husband."

That seems to appease him because he melts into my side. He has one arm around my back and the other on my knee. I'm surrounded by him, but I appreciate the sense of protection it gives me.

"Do you know what you're having?" The woman across from me gestures to my belly.

I smile. "A girl. We're having a girl."

Her smile brightens. "Me too."

I look at the vacant seat next to the woman and worry that she's here by herself. As if reading my mind, she shrugs her shoulders. "My husband had to work."

I nod. "Have you picked out a name yet?"

That seems to perk the woman up. She starts to talk, and I sit here quietly, listening to her talk about baby names, when the baby's due, and how she's a little scared because this is her first child.

I ask her questions and encourage her to talk, sensing that she needs to. When the nurse calls my name, I impulsively hug the woman. I knew it was the right thing to do when I pull back and she's beaming at me yet wiping a tear from her eye. "Thank you," she says. "I'm sorry to have talked you and your husband's ear off."

I shake my head. "You didn't. I enjoyed meeting you."

After a few brief exchanges, Austin and I walk through the doors for our appointment. He's watching me closely, and I try to focus on the questions the nurse is asking me. I go into the bathroom to give a sample and then find myself in the room with Austin as we wait for the doctors.

As soon as I walk into the room, Austin hands me a thin tissue-like blanket. "You know the drill."

I take it from his hands and lay it on the bed. The last few visits, they've had me undress from the waist down to examine me. Austin helps me with my shoes and then removing my pants and underwear. He takes my hand and helps me up onto the bed. He positions the thin blanket around me and then puts his hands on the bed, next to my hips. "That was nice of you out there. That woman needed that."

I shrug, acting like it didn't bother me, but it did. The truth is, I can see myself in that woman. If it wasn't for Austin, I would be here by myself, and I would probably latch on to the first person that was willing to hear me talk too.

Austin puts his hand over mine. "Have you picked out a name?"

I bite my lower lip. "Yeah, but I'd like to make sure you're okay with it."

His forehead creases in confusion. "Okay?"

"Kennedy," I blurt out and hold my breath.

He points a thumb at himself. "You want to give her my middle name?"

I hold my hands up, unable to tell what he's thinking. "I don't have to. I've always liked your middle name. It's a good name. And you're my best friend... I just thought...."

My voice trails off, and he cups my face in his hands. "It's perfect. You're perfect. I'm honored that you would pick my name, Ally."

He looks so unsure. Almost as if he doesn't think he's deserving or something. I bring my hand up and press it to his chest, right over his heart. The steady thud against my palm calms me. "Austin, you've been a huge part of my life forever. You've taken care of me." I grab his hand and put it over my belly. "And my daughter. No matter what happens in the future, I want her to always have a piece of you."

He sucks in a breath and opens his mouth to say something but closes it when there's a knock on the door. Austin straightens and moves to my side, wrapping his hand around mine again. "Come in," he says huskily.

The door opens, and both Dr. Parks and Dr. Reynolds come in. We've been coming every week, and I had assumed this appointment would be like the others, but they both have worried looks on their faces. "How are you feeling?" Dr. Parks asks.

At the same time, I see Dr. Reynolds give Austin an apologetic look.

I sit up straighter. "What is it? What's going on?"

Dr. Parks doesn't make me wait. "There is protein in your urine, and your blood pressure is elevated." I open my mouth, but he stops me. "It's going to be okay. The last thing we need is for you to stress out. This is what's going to happen. We're going to examine you and check the baby, and then we're going to make a decision on what happens next. Okay?"

The older doctor is patient and pats me on the shoulder.

Austin helps me lie back, and I put my feet in the stirrups. With my eyes closed, I try not to worry, but it's a waste of time because every scenario is running through my head.

"Have you been having any contractions?"

"No," Austin answers at the same time as I say, "Yeah, but I thought for sure they were Braxton-Hicks."

Austin gives me a look, and I grab his shirt, just wanting to touch him. "I didn't want to bother you—"

He leans over and kisses me on the lips and then presses his forehead to mine. "What am I going to do with you?"

The doctor finishes the examination and then

gets out the wand.

Austin and I both stare at the screen, waiting to see little Kennedy.

When the baby appears and her heartbeat fills the room, I let out a breath of relief. She's moving around, and it looks as if she's sucking on her thumb.

Dr. Reynolds takes a few pictures and then hands me some tissues.

Austin and I both clean me up and then he helps me sit up.

Dr. Parks says, "We're going to let you get dressed and let's meet in my office, okay?"

"Okay," I stutter out.

Austin is my rock. He helps me get dressed, even putting on my socks and tennis shoes. He helps me from the table and wraps his arm around me, tucking me against his side as we make our way to Dr. Parks' office. Before we walk through the doors, Austin kisses my forehead again. "Everything's going to be okay."

I nod as he opens the door and we walk in. We take our seats, and Dr. Parks is sitting behind his desk, while Dr. Reynolds is leaning against another desk. Dr. Reynolds is the first to speak. "First of all, I want you to know that everything is okay. Things are going to happen fast, but I just want you to know that you and the baby are okay."

I gulp and tighten my hand in Austin's. "O-okay," I stutter.

Dr. Parks leans back in his seat and brings his hands together. "So your blood pressure is elevated, and you're already dilated to three cm. Also, since there is protein in your urine, we would like to go ahead and induce labor."

My mouth drops. "Now?"

He nods his head. "Yes."

I shake my head. "But we have another month."

"The baby is thirty-five weeks and is already measuring almost six and a half pounds."

I look at Austin, who looks at Dr. Reynolds. "And you both agree that this—"

Brandon cuts him off. "Yes, it's best for Ally and the baby." He smiles. "You are going to be a mom and dad by the end of the day."

To hear him say it like that, a shudder goes through me. I understand it has to happen, but all I can think and pray about is that my baby is going to be okay. She has to be. "Okay, whatever you think is best, let's do that."

As soon as I get the words out, things go pretty quickly. They bring in a wheelchair, and Austin wheels me through the corridors that connect to the hospital. We ride the elevator to the maternity floor, and I'm in a gown and on the hospital bed in no time at all.

Austin is standing over me. "I have to tell my brothers. They'll never forgive me if not."

I nod my head. "Do you think they'll want to come?"

He laughs. "Do I think they'll want to come and meet their niece? Absolutely." He holds his hand up. "But I promise, I'll make them wait out in the lobby until after she's born. Up until then, it's just me and you, but after that, there's no promises. Kennedy is going to have four aunts and uncles and a cousin that is going to be vying for her attention."

He's attempting to warn me, but all it does is fill my chest with a warm, cozy feeling. The Blazes are my family now, and the tears that start to fill my eyes are because I know that no matter what, Kennedy is going to have a family that accepts her and loves her as their own. "Thank you, Austin. Not just for everything you do for me and Kennedy but also for how you make me feel. The fact you were having one of your guest bedrooms made into a nursery before I even moved in tells me a lot. Thank you for..." I suck in a breath, knowing the words are not enough. "For everything."

He kisses me then. I put my hand at the back of his head because I don't want it to end. In his arms, I feel that everything is going to be all right. He is my calm, and I don't ever want to let him go.

Chapter 24

Austin

It's been a whirlwind few days. My brothers all stepped in like I knew they would. They brought our overnight bags to the hospital and agreed to stay in the waiting room until after little Kennedy was born. Ally was amazing. She gave birth at noon and was up walking around that night. The doctors kept both Ally and Kennedy a few days for observation. They wanted to make sure that Ally was completely healthy before releasing her, and even though I had to sleep on a lumpy chair, I didn't mind. I would stay as long as we needed to if it meant keeping Ally healthy.

By the third day, when both were given a clean bill of health, I packed up our little family and drove us home.

Ally is sleeping in our bedroom, and I'm sitting in the nursery, holding Kennedy to my chest. She started cooing a few minutes ago, so I thought I'd pick her up and let Ally get some more rest, but the way she's squirming, it's obvious she doesn't want to wait any longer.

I carry her to the next room, and Ally lifts her head. "I'm sorry, I should have gotten her."

I laugh. "Why would you do that? Kennedy and I had some daddy-daughter time, and we've already decided that she's not going to date until she's twenty. Isn't that a relief?"

Ally laughs. Her red hair is in tangles around her head, and she smiles at me. "Oh yes, what a relief. I can't believe she agreed to it."

I position the baby at Ally's chest. She's lost all modesty since she became a mom, and all I can do is sit here and stare as Kennedy suckles at her chest.

The need to touch Ally is overwhelming, and I reach over, lifting her up so I can sit down behind her and then let her lean back into my chest. She sighs as she rests against me. This is the life that I've always hoped for and thought I'd never have. I'm determined to soak it all in.

The vibration of the phone on the nightstand startles us. "It's yours," I whisper to her.

She groans, but it's obvious she's smiling. "It's probably Natalie or Elle, and if I don't answer, they're going to have your brothers call you to check on us."

I reach for the phone and pick it up, ready to answer to one of my sisters-in-law but am surprised when I see the name on the caller ID.

"Who is it?" Ally asks me.

"It's Gregory," I answer and hate myself for doing so because I can feel her whole body tense.

I answer the phone, keeping my voice nice and soft even though I feel anything but. "What?"

There is silence on the other end of the phone. "Uh, may I speak to Alison?"

I grit my teeth and keep my voice low. I hate even hearing him say her name. "She can't come to the phone. Not now, not ever."

"Uh, I have some legal matters to talk to her about. Or I could just send a police officer over there."

"Hold on," I grunt at him.

I put the phone on mute. Forcing myself to relax, I kiss Ally on the side of her neck. "It's going to be okay. I'm going out. I'm going to have Elle and Huddy come over, okay?"

I get up from the bed with the phone held tightly

in my hand. I lean over and kiss the top of Kennedy's head and then kiss Ally. "I promise, everything's going to be all right."

Ally grabs on to me. "Austin, please don't do anything."

I force a smile. "It's going to be okay. I'll be back in a few hours."

I wait until I'm out of the room and then unmute the phone. "Do you know who you're talking to?"

He chuckles. "Austin, I know exactly who I'm talking to, and I'm not scared of you. The fact is that is my baby, and I have rights."

I grit my jaw. "You want to talk about your rights? Meet me at 1201 Main Street in one hour. Don't be late. We'll talk about your rights."

I hang up the phone and then start making calls. First to Huddy. He promises me that he and Elle are on their way.

Then I send a text to my attorney and tell him to have "surrender" papers prepared and that I'll be there in an hour.

I then call Ford because I don't want to piss him off again. I know he can't do anything in this situation, but I at least need to let him know what's up. "What's up, Daddy?"

I let out a disgusted groan. "Please don't ever call

me that again. It's just so weird coming out of your mouth."

He chuckles. "Fine, Poppa, what's up?"

I groan. "Hey, I just wanted to fill you in on what's going on. Kennedy's biological father called and wants to establish his fatherly rights."

"Fuck!" Ford says, and I couldn't agree more.

"Yeah, I know. Anyway, I'm meeting him at Brian's in an hour to try and convince him to surrender his rights."

"What can I do?"

I peek out the front door, wondering where Huddy's at. "Nothing. I just didn't want to leave you out of the loop or anything. He threatened sending the cops over here, so I'm having Elle and Huddy come over and stay with Ally and Kennedy. I just wanted..."

He cuts me off. "I got it, brother. I'll meet you there."

I'm about to tell him he doesn't have to come, that I can handle it myself, but there's a part of me that feels better knowing my big brother will be there too. I let out a sigh. "Thanks, Ford. I appreciate it."

I hang up the phone, and Huddy is pulling in on two wheels in my driveway. He no sooner parks than he's out of the truck and around to the passenger door to help Elle out. She walks up to me and puts a hand on my shoulder. "Where's Ally?"

"Up in the bedroom."

She nods and walks in the front door. Huddy walks up to me, and the look he gives me is intense. "Okay, ready?"

I put my hand on his shoulder. "I need you to stay here, Huddy."

He shakes his head. "Fuck that, I'm coming with you."

I put my hands on my hips. "Huddy, Gregory said he was sending the cops over here. I don't know whether I believe him or not, but I'm not taking any chances. I need you to stay here and make sure no one gets near Ally or Kennedy. I need to know they're both okay so I can do this."

He blows out a breath and cracks his knuckles. Huddy, after years in the military, is more of an action guy, and I know he'll hate sitting here, but I also know that he won't let anyone get inside that's not supposed to.

He finally nods his head. "Okay. Fine, I got it."

I hug him, and he wraps me up tightly before releasing me. "Take care of this, Austin. Ally and that little girl are Blazes, and no one messes with a Blaze."

I nod. "I got it."

I drive into town and pull up in front of the attorney's building. I'm the first to arrive, and I bypass the secretary and go straight into the office. "You got it? Everything ready?"

He pushes his glasses up his nose and looks at me. "Did you doubt me?"

I shake my head. "No, I'm sorry. I'm just on edge, that's all."

"It's understandable. But yes, all the papers are ready. I can make any changes you deem necessary."

I grab the paperwork and read through it briefly. Once I see the paragraph about Gregory giving up all rights with no future claims, then I stop reading because I know Brian has everything else correct. He's been our family's attorney forever, and I completely trust him.

The intercom buzzes, and Brian's secretary's voice fills the room. "You have a Gregory Harper here to see you."

Brian touches the button on his phone. "Send him in." When he rises to his full height, he's straightening his tie. "You ready for this?"

I nod as Gregory walks in the door. He looks around the room. "Where is Alison?"

I cross my arms over my chest. "Alison is at home. You're meeting with me."

He has one hand on the door, and I'm afraid he's about to step out when I spot Ford behind him. Ford, Lucas, and Beau all walk in, effectively shoving Gregory into the center of the room.

He looks around the room, and I swear he shrinks two feet in size. He starts to stutter. "What.. I wanted to.. uh, meet with..."

I cut him off. "Don't say her name. Don't even think about her. We're married now. She's my wife."

His face scrunches up. "You are not, that's a damn lie."

I laugh. "Believe what you want, but just know that you won't ever upset her again. I don't want you to say her name. Hell, I don't want you to think about her. You won't contact her, call her, or reach out to her in any way. She doesn't want to see you."

He's angry, but he's trying to rein it in. "And my daughter... if I can't contact Ali—"

I take a step toward him, and he changes his words up. "How do I see my daughter if I can't contact her mother?"

"You won't be seeing our daughter either."

His hands fist at his side. "She's not yours... she's—"

"Don't say it," I tell him. There's no way I can stand here while he claims my daughter as his. "This is how it's going to go. Brian here has the papers for you to sign."

He shakes his head. "I'm not signing anything."

I just laugh. "Oh, trust me, you're signing."

His jaw is tight, and I'm surprised that he's fighting me on this. I'm already over this conversation, and I want it to end. "How much?"

His eyebrows almost disappear in his hair line. "How much?"

I nod. "Yeah, how much, and don't act like you want to be in the baby's life. We both know you don't."

He looks at me and then around at my brothers. They're each standing with their feet shoulder length apart and arms crossed over their chests. I know exactly what he sees when he looks at us. It's almost like the dollar signs are glaring from his eyes.

He tilts his head to the side. "You're willing to pay me to stay out of the baby's life?"

I correct him. "Out of Ally and Kennedy's life."

His voice is strangled, and it's obvious he's excited. "How much?"

"Two hundred thousand."

He rolls his eyes. "Please, don't insult me."

I just laugh. "Really, if you ask me, this is the easy way. We can walk out of here, and in the next few weeks or so, we can arrange to have you audited. I'm sure they'll find everything with your marketing business is on the up and up, right?"

He juts his chin at me. "Two hundred and fifty thousand."

"Done. Sign the paper and give Brian your account information. It will be in your account by the end of the day. Make sure you read it all. You are to have no interaction with Ally or Kennedy."

He briefly glances through the papers and then signs them. "I knew I would be able to make you pay. I didn't want anything to do with them anyway."

I reach for him, but Ford stops me. "He's not worth it, Austin. He's signed the papers, and now he's never going to step foot in Whiskey Run again. If he does, he'll have all of us to deal with."

Gregory looks at each of my brothers, and I know we're an intimidating bunch. "Understood."

As soon as Brian hands him copies of what he just signed, Gregory walks out the door.

Each of my brothers congratulate me, and I accept their hugs, but I'm ready to get out of here. I want to hold my wife and my daughter.

Chapter 25

Ally

I appreciate what Elle and Huddy are trying to do. They've kept me occupied and done their best to keep my mind off things, but all I can think about is Austin. I wouldn't be surprised in the least if he came home and said he was done and that I'm more trouble than I'm worth. But even thinking it, I know it won't happen.

Finally, around three hours after Austin left, I hear him coming in through the garage door. I'm out of my seat and run toward him without even thinking. Kennedy is safe in Elle's arms, freeing me to act on impulse.

As soon as he clears the doorway, I dive for him. He catches me easily, pulling me up in his arms. "Hey, hey, I'm okay. Everything's okay."

I breathe out a sigh of relief. "I'm just so glad you're home. I've been so worried."

He picks me up and carries me over to the recliner. He sits down, cradling me in his lap. I should be embarrassed, but I'm not in the least. If anything, I curl into him and relish the feel of his arms around me.

Austin looks around at his brother and sister-in-law and back at me. "He signed the papers. We won't ever have to see him again."

"But what about—?"

He cuts me off. "No, there are no buts. He has signed over all his rights. He can never have any claim on Kennedy. The attorney included you. He can't talk to you, either."

I lay my head on his chest. Elle, Huddy, and Austin all talk around me, but I tune it all out. All that matters to me is that Kennedy is mine, and Gregory can never take her from me.

Elle walks over to me and places Kennedy on my chest. I thank her and Huddy, and they leave after telling us to call if we need anything.

"Tell me the truth, Austin. You asked him to sign the papers and he just signed them? It was that easy?"

"I gave him money."

I lift my head up. "Wait, what? You gave him money?"

He nods his head. "Ally, he wasn't walking out of there without signing those papers."

"How much money did you have to give him?"

He brushes my hair off my face. "It doesn't matter."

I sit up in his arms, holding a sleeping Kennedy against my chest. "Yes, it does. How much?"

"Two hundred and fifty thousand."

My mouth gapes, and I mouth the words. *Two hundred and fifty thousand.* I tap his chest with my free hand. "Austin, I'm so sorry. I can't—"

He leans forward and presses his lips to my forehead. "If you're about to say something about paying me back, you'd better keep it to yourself. I told you that I would protect you and Kennedy, and I meant it."

Speechless, I don't know what to say or do. A thousand thoughts race through my head, but I don't put voice to any of them.

Austin runs his fingers softly against Kennedy's cheek. "Can you lay her down? I think we need to talk."

I suck in a sob, having an idea of what this is about. It's like my thoughts are becoming reality, and he's going to tell me that this is too much for him. I struggle from his lap and carry Kennedy over to the bassinet by the couch. I lean over, breathing in her sweet, innocent scent before moving back over to the couch and sitting down on the edge of it. "What do you want to talk about?"

Austin is pacing back and forth in front of me, and the more he does it, the more nervous I get. "Austin, stop. What is it? You're scaring me."

He stops in front of me and looks at me before sitting down next to me. He brushes his hand through my hair. "You're so damn beautiful, Ally."

I smile and laugh. "Okay, that doesn't sound so bad."

I put my hand on his forearm and feel the swell of his muscles from my touch. He covers my hand with his own and squeezes. "Like I said, I need to tell you something."

"Okay. I'm ready."

He clears his throat. "I love you, Ally."

I feel the warmth of a blush cross my cheeks. "I love you, too, Austin."

He shakes his head and scoots closer to me. "No, I mean, I love you. I've loved you forever. Since we were younger, I've wanted to be your man."

I scoot back from him. "Don't lie to me, Austin."

He lets his hand fall from mine as he breathes out. "I'm not. I'm not lying to you. All these years, I've wished we could be more."

My hand curls into a fist in my lap. "But why didn't you say anything? Why didn't you tell me?"

It almost looks like heartbreak in his smile. "Because I couldn't give you the one thing you always wanted."

I search his face and start to stutter. "What... but...What are you talking about? What is it that you think you couldn't give me?"

He looks over at Kennedy, and his face softens, but his words are hard and regretful. "I couldn't give you a child, Ally."

"What? What do you mean?"

He shakes his head and looks down at his hands in his lap. "Remember in high school and I got hurt our sophomore year?"

I try to recall all those years ago. "In the baseball game?"

He nods. "Yeah, it was worse than I let on. I'm unable to..."

He lets his voice trail off, but I get the gist of what he's telling me. "But I don't understand... what does that have to do with you and me?"

He lifts his eyes to mine. "Ally, forever you

talked about wanting to have a family of your own. You talked about getting pregnant and having kids, and I knew I couldn't do that for you even though I wanted it more than anything. I thought I was doing the right thing, and I did, because there's no denying you having Kennedy is worth it."

I shake my head, not understanding. "But I don't get it. It doesn't make sense. If this was true, Austin, then you wouldn't have asked me to marry you. You wouldn't have insisted we get married."

His whole body shudders as he begins to talk. "I thought I was being a good friend by standing to the side while you dated other men. I wanted you to be happy, but fuck, Ally, knowing you were with another man, knowing that I could lose you forever, I couldn't do it. I was selfish, and I know I should have told you all this before I practically forced you to marry me, but I didn't."

I'm quiet, trying to collect my thoughts, knowing that what I'm about to say could change any and everything between us.

Chapter 26

Austin

She's going to end it. She's going to walk away from me, and I'll never survive it. I go to my knees on the floor in front of her. "Listen to me Ally. I love you, and I know you don't feel the same. I know I went about this all wrong, but I want you to be happy. I figure you have two options."

She juts her chin at me. "Oh yeah, two options, huh? Well, since you seem to have my whole life mapped out, please tell me what my two options are."

She's mad. I knew she would be. Ally and I have always been honest with each other, and I knew she wouldn't take it well that I had lied to her all these years.

There's a pain in my chest, and I know it's from my heart breaking in two. "So no matter which option you choose, you have to know that you and Ally will be cared for. Gregory is out of the picture, and he won't give you any problems."

She crosses her arms over her chest. I want to pull her into my arms, but I resist. "Option one, you divorce me. You can live in a house down the street, and I'll still be here for you and Kennedy."

She snarls her nose up at me, and I continue. "Option two, you stay married to me. You let me prove to you for the rest of our lives how much I love you and how important your happiness is to me. You let me be Kennedy's father for real. And when you want more children down the road, we can adopt or whatever you want to do."

She leans forward. "So you're giving me an option."

I nod but then shake my head no. I wanted to be the bigger man. I want to put her choices before my own, but the fear of her leaving me is too much to handle. "Fuck, I want to, Ally. I want you to have what you want, but the truth is, I can't let you and Kennedy go. You have one option and that option is me. If you need time, I can give you that, but I can't let you go. Please don't ask me to."

She shoots to her feet and stands over me. I rise from my crouched position, and the fear that she's about to walk away from me has me grabbing her arms to hold her still. The look she's giving me makes it impossible to know what she's thinking.

"Ally, talk to me, please."

She raises her eyes and levels me with a look. "I want to be mad at you for lying to me, for thinking that you weren't enough to make me happy. I want to be mad about all the time that we wasted, but I can't."

"You can't?"

She shakes her head and points at the bassinet. "If things were different, we wouldn't have Kennedy, and we both know that even though it took us down different paths, we made it to here. We have each other, we have our daughter. I can't be mad at you because I have to believe that all of this happened for a reason."

I reach for her, plucking the hem of her shirt and pulling her toward me. "And future babies? What about them? Are you going to resent me, Ally?"

She reaches for me, cupping my jaw in her hand. "You fool. I could never resent you. I love our little family, and if it's meant for us to have more, it will happen. How doesn't matter to me. All that matters is I have you now, and I don't want to let you go." She takes a deep breath and lets it out slowly. "Two. I would have chosen option two."

She barely gets the words out before I pull her to me, wrapping my arms around her lush body. She burrows into me, and I kiss the top of her head. "Fuck, I love you, Ally. I always have and I always will."

She lifts her eyes and looks into mine. "I love you, Austin. I always have and I always will."

Our lips meet, and I ravage her mouth, putting every emotion I've felt today into this one kiss. She tilts her head to the side, and I deepen the kiss, wanting to consume her. I could get lost in us until I hear Kennedy's soft whimper.

Ally raises her head to look at me. Her lips are swollen, and her hair is mussed. She glances at the baby and then back at me. "I'm sorry. I should feed her."

I nod. "Don't ever apologize to me, Ally. We have forever. Have a seat. I'll bring her to you."

She sits down, and I go pick up Kennedy. Feelings erupt inside me as I hold Kennedy in my arms. With her and Ally in my life, I want to be a better man... the best man.

I kiss Kennedy's head and then place her in her mom's arms. She was waiting for her, and she holds her to her breast. Kennedy immediately latches on, and I sit and pull Ally against me. I don't take lightly the fact that I have my whole heart in my arms.

Epilogue

Ally

I get home from the salon and rush through the door. I was hoping to get home before Kennedy went to sleep, but I know I didn't make it.

After kicking my shoes off at the front door, I drop my purse on the kitchen counter and make my way up the stairs, practically sprinting to the nursery. But once I'm in the doorway, I stop in my tracks.

Austin is sitting in the rocking chair, holding a sleeping Kennedy against his bare chest. I could watch them together for hours. I have done just that plenty of times.

I lean into the doorway with my arms crossed over my chest.

Austin's eyes slowly open, and he smiles at me.

With a whisper, he says, "You're home. I tried to keep her awake, but she wasn't having it."

I nod. "It's okay. This is the only day I'm working this week. I'm okay," I reassure him. Over and over, he's told me he'd support me in whatever decision I made. He didn't care if I never worked another day in my life, or if I chose to go back to my regular schedule, he would support me. The decision was mine. In the end, I knew I didn't want to be away from Kennedy—or him—all the time, so I made the decision to only work one day a week. However, this time, that one day was literally all day.

I whisper to him, "How was it spending all day with a baby? Are YOU doing okay?"

He shrugs, and I have to admit he looks completely refreshed and happy. "I'm fine. My brothers all took turns coming today, so Kennedy and I have been pretty busy." He looks at me sheepishly. "Plus, Natalie, Elle, and Isabella came by, so yeah, I pretty much just sat here all day." He gestures to Kennedy in his arms. "And she, the little traitor, ate it up. I thought for sure she'd hate having my brothers or the girls holding her, but nooooo, she enjoyed every minute of it."

I move into the room and sit on the arm of the chair. "You're jealous."

He shrugs. "Yeah, I am. But also, it feels good. This little girl has a lot of people that love her."

I put my hand to my chest. "Yes, yes she does."

Austin leans his head against me. "Also, just so you know, Natalie went into labor."

I jump up from the arm of the chair and look at him. "What? Austin, we need to be there, right? We should go. Or you should go."

He shakes his head and stands up from the chair. He kisses the top of Kennedy's head before laying her in her crib. When he stands up, he reaches for me. "We should go, but I already told them that we'd be there tomorrow. When we get up, we'll go."

It doesn't feel right. "Austin, your family is..."

He interrupts me. "My family is right here."

I put my hand to his chest, letting his words breeze over me. It's always amazing to me that he can just use his words to soothe me.

He wraps his hand around mine and threads our fingers together. I pull his hand into my lap and run my other finger along the back of his hand. "So, is this how you thought you'd be spending your Friday nights?"

He releases my hand and then brings his fingers up to my face. I tilt my head into his hands. "Are you asking me if I thought I'd be spending my Friday nights with my daughter against my chest? Or that I'd be waiting at home, counting down the minutes until my beautiful wife and best friend would come home and look at me as if I just hung the moon?" He smirks and shakes his head. "No, Ally, I dreamed of this. I wanted this more than anything I've ever wanted in my life, but no, I never let myself believe I would have it. You made my life what it is, and it's perfect."

I brush my hands through his hair. "God, I love you, Austin. I'm not sure what I did to deserve you, but I'll never take you for granted."

He nods. "I love you, too, baby." He gestures to the baby. "What about you? Did you think you'd be spending your Friday nights like this?"

I shrug. "Well, the book club is talking about the next field trip, and they're going to a sex club."

I try to hold back my smirk, waiting for his response, and he doesn't disappoint. "You're not going to a sex club without me."

I laugh and shake my head. "I have everything I want right here, Austin."

I tug on his hand. "I'm going to bed. You going to join me?"

I wiggle my eyebrows at him, and his nose flairs. "Yeah, baby, I'm coming."

I kiss Kennedy on the head and then skip out of the nursery. One of my favorite parts of every day is when I'm lying in Austin's arms. I know it was a long time getting here, but it was worth it. We are worth it.

Also by Hope Ford

Want more of Whiskey Run?

Whiskey Run

Faithful - He's the hot, say-it-like-it-is cowboy, and he won't stop until he gets the woman he wants.

Captivated - She's a beautiful woman on the run... and I'm going to be the one to keep her.

Obsessed - She's loved him since high school and now he's back.

Seduced - He's a football player that falls in love with the small town girl.

Devoted - She's a plus size model and he's a small town mechanic.

Whiskey Run: Savage Ink

Virile - He won't let her go until he puts his mark on her.

Torrid - He'll do anything to give her what she wants.

Rigid - If you love reading about emotionally wounded men and the women that help them overcome their past, then you'll love Dawson and Emily's story.

Whiskey Run: Cowboys Love Curves

Obsessed Cowboy - She's the preacher's daughter and she's

off limits.

Whiskey Run: Heroes

Ransom - He's on a mission he can't lose.

Redeem - He's in love with his sister's best friend.

Submit - She's his fake wife but he wants to make it real.

Forbid - They have a secret romance but he's about to stake his claim.

Whiskey Run: Sugar

One Night Love - Her one night stand wants more.

Rebound Love - She's falling for the rebound guy.

Second Chance Love - He is not a man to ignore... especially when he asks for a second chance.

Bad Boy Love - He's a bad boy that wants her good.

Whiskey Run: Guardians MC

Protective Biker - She needs his protection and he'll give it to her. But he's going to need her heart in exchange.

Broken Biker - There's only one woman for him...

Relentless Biker - He won't stop until he has her back.

Whiskey Men

Reluctant Husband - If you love reading about curvy women getting the hot guy, opposites attract, jealousy trope, marriage of convenience, and small-town romance, then you'll love Lucas and Isabella's story.

Something Real - If you love reading billionaire, single father, age gap, boss/employee, and small-town romance, then you'll love Ford and Lilian's story.

Coming Home - If you love reading billionaire, ex-military, age gap, forced proximity, and small-town romance, then you'll love Hudson and Elle's story.

Forever Mine - If you love reading billionaire, age gap, second chance, and small-town romance, then you'll love Beau and Natalie's story.

Always Yours - If you love reading billionaire, friends to lovers, pregnancy, and small town romance, then you'll love Austin and Ally's story.

JOIN ME!

JOIN MY NEWSLETTER

www.AuthorHopeFord.com/Subscribe

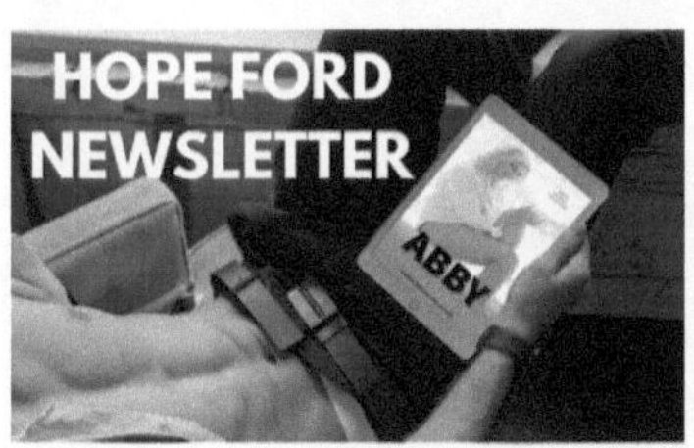

Be a Hottie!

JOIN HOPE'S HOTTIES ON FACEBOOK

www.FB.com/groups/hopeford

A place to talk about Hope Ford's books! Find out about new releases, giveaways, get exclusive content, see covers before anyone else and more!

About the Author

USA Today Bestselling Author Hope Ford writes short, steamy, sweet romances. She loves tattooed, alpha men, instant love stories, and ALWAYS happily ever afters. She has over 100 books and they are all available on Amazon.

To find me on Pinterest, Instagram, Facebook, Goodreads, and more:

www.AuthorHopeFord.com/follow-me

Want FREE BOOKS?
Go to www.authorhopeford.com/freebies